I couldn't have felt more so...
I read more than my fair ...
make me keep the light on ...
lots of books that make me sad, or anxious, till things work out right. But I don't end up in a state like her, halfway to fainting because of three or four grisly pages, and not even able to look at the cover of that book again without wanting to shudder.

'A gift', her mother called it. But, the more Imogen told me about it, the more I thought that that was totally the wrong word.

'Curse' was more like it.

Yes. Not 'gift', but 'curse' . . .

Bad Dreams

Anne Fine

Illustrated by Susan Winter

CORGI YEARLING BOOKS

CHARM SCHOOL AND BAD DREAMS
A CORGI YEARLING BOOK 0 552 55405 7

This edition first published in Great Britain for Scholastic by Corgi Yearling,
an imprint of Random House Children s Books, 2005

1 3 5 7 9 10 8 6 4 2

CHARM SCHOOL
First published in Great Britain by Doubleday, 1999
Copyright ' Anne Fine, 1999
Illustrations copyright ' Ros Asquith, 1999

BAD DREAMS
First published in Great Britain by Doubleday, 2000
Copyright ' Anne Fine, 2000
Illustrations copyright ' Susan Winter, 2000

The right of Anne Fine to be identified as the author of this work has been
asserted in accordance with the Copyright, Designs and Patents Act 1988.

Corgi Yearling Books are published by Random House Children s Books,
61—63 Uxbridge Road, London W5 5SA,
a division of The Random House Group Ltd,
in Australia by Random House Australia (Pty) Ltd,
20 Alfred Street, Milsons Point, Sydney, NSW 2061, Australia,
in New Zealand by Random House New Zealand Ltd,
18 Poland Road, Glenfield, Auckland 10, New Zealand,
and in South Africa by Random House (Pty) Ltd,
Endulini, 5A Jubilee Road, Parktown 2193, South Africa

THE RANDOM HOUSE GROUP Limited Reg. No. 954009
www.kidsatrandomhouse.co.uk

A CIP catalogue record for this book is available from the British Library.

Printed and bound in Great Britain by
Cox & Wyman Ltd, Reading, Berkshire

For Jon Appleton,
without whom . . .

CHAPTER ONE

It's only been bothering me a tiny bit. But still, Mr Hooper saw my uneasy look.

'What ho, Mel!' he offered. 'A trouble shared is a trouble halved?'

I shook my head. 'No, thanks. It's too private.'

'Write it down, then,' he told me. 'If something's gnawing at you, shove it on paper.'

I waved at the books round us, shelf upon shelf of them, up to the ceiling.

'Is that what the writers of some of these were doing?'

'Quite a few, I should think,' he said. 'False

names, true stories, and they make a mint. You try it. I'll buy a copy.'

He went off chuckling and I sat down to think. Why not? I'm good at stories. I could call it *Bad Dreams*. Or even, *Imogen Imagines*, since it would be about her, and how she came to our school and spooked all of us – especially me – with her weirdness, and all of her horrible imaginings.

This is how it started. She turned up halfway through one morning in summer term. She came through the doorway behind Mrs Trent, who simply handed her over and left in a hurry.

Mr Hooper had only the briefest of chats with her at the desk before turning to the rest of us. 'Class, this is Imogen Tate, who's joining us from another school.'

She looked embarrassed, and we stared. She was already dressed in our boring old school uniform, with her hair in plain bunches. There was absolutely nothing special about her, but in spite of that everyone wanted to be her first-week minder. Almost all of them put their hands up.

But Mr Hooper said, 'And I pick – Melanie!'

I was astonished. *Me?*

'Well,' he said, 'why not?'

'I didn't put my hand up.'

'That doesn't matter,' he said. 'It'll be nice for

you to have someone in that empty seat.'

I didn't think so, but I couldn't say. Maybe I should explain. I'm the class bookworm. I don't mix much with the others because I like reading better. All the way up the school it's bothered my teachers. One after another, they've tried to prise the books out of my hands, and get me to join in more.

Yet I still prefer reading.

But you can't be rude to someone who's new, and standing there trembling. So I just patted the spare chair at my side, and she came over. And as she was busy unpacking her pens and pencils into the desk, I finally thought of something friendly to say.

'I like that necklace you're wearing. Is it gold?'
She nodded shyly.

'*Real* gold?'

'Yes,' she said. 'My granny gave it to my mother, and now it's been passed down to me.'

I peered at it more closely. It had strange little scratchy markings, and looked fine and slinky enough to be spilled into a teaspoon.

'You're so lucky,' I told her, still trying to be nice. 'I'm sure no-one will ever pass anything special down to me.'

As if I'd suddenly reminded her of something, she stopped in the middle of her unpacking and gave me a look. 'Then maybe you're the lucky one,' she told me.

I stared at her. 'What do you mean?'

She wouldn't say. In fact, she hardly said anything at all after that, except things like, 'Should I write this in the red book?' and, 'Do I use pen or pencil to do this?' and, 'Can I borrow your ruler?'

I bet she didn't even realize that what she'd said stuck in my mind. But it was like the first clue in a book. It just stuck out. And it was *strange*.

CHAPTER TWO

S he was no good at schoolwork. You could tell Mr Hooper was amazed how badly she did in all the tests he set her. But he still made her book monitor, along with me.

'Since Melly's looking after you,' he explained.

'Must I?' she asked him. 'I hate books.'

I was astonished. 'Hate them? Actually *hate* them?'

She blushed. 'Well,' she said, 'I just don't get on with them very well.'

What can you say? I love books more than anything. Left to myself, I wouldn't come to school at all. I'd spend my whole life reading. 'Go out,' my mother tells me. 'It's lovely today. Go and play in the fresh air.' But I'd rather stay in my bedroom, and read about other children going out to play.

'You're not a bit like me, then,' I told Imogen. 'You know those battered old Christmas albums you see in jumble sales that have a picture on the front of a girl reading another album just the same, with a picture of herself on the cover? You know how they go on, down and down, smaller and smaller, like boxes inside boxes, until the girl's too small to be seen?'

'Yes, I've seen those.'

'Well,' I said, 'that's who I want to be. That girl who's reading all the other lives in from the outside.'

Now it was her turn to look at me as if I were loopy. 'Really?'

'Yes,' I admitted. 'That's who I'd like to be more than anyone in the world.'

And then I showed her how to use the card index in the book corner. And how to stamp the books out, and how to tell from the coloured sticker on the spine whether it should go back in Older Readers, or Poetry, or Project Work.

She had a funny way of picking up the books – gingerly, as if they might scorch her. After a few minutes, I asked her, as a joke:

'Didn't you have any of these in your old school?'

She made a face. 'Oh, yes,' she said. 'We had them. It's just that I hardly ever had to go near them.'

Strange thing to say. And I was just thinking, 'No wonder her work's so bad', when, suddenly, I saw her jump.

'Oh!' she said, startled.

'What's the matter?'

'Nothing.'

But I couldn't help noticing she hadn't touched that book again. She was staring at it nervously.

'It's that book, isn't it?' I said. 'Something about it has upset you.'

'Don't be silly,' she said. But she had definitely gone red again.

I'm not an idiot. I kept a watch. And only a few minutes later, I saw it happen a second time. Imogen picked up a different book, and dropped it as if it had stung her.

As if it were red hot.

13

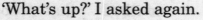

'What's up?' I asked again.

'Nothing.'

I think, when people try to fool you, they can practically expect you to start spying on them. And that's why I was watching so closely when, later that morning, Mr Hooper hurried past her without a single word, then, noticing her anxious little 'new-girl' face, stopped guiltily and thrust the book he happened to be carrying into her hand.

'Here, Imogen,' he said. 'You say you don't like books. Try this one – *Violet's Game*. Melly says it's brilliant. It's about a girl called Violet. That's her you can see on the cover, cuddling that kitten. And she—'

He broke off because Imogen was already backing away. 'Oh, no! I couldn't bear it! I can't stand stories about animals that have been hurt.'

Mr Hooper looked a bit surprised. 'Sorry,' he said. 'I hadn't realized you'd already read it.'

'Oh, no.' Imogen started to shake her head, then stopped, embarrassed. And Mr Hooper looked a little embarrassed, too. After all, just because *Violet's Game* has only just come into our class book corner, it didn't mean Imogen couldn't have come across it back in her old school.

'Well, at least it ends happily,' Mr Hooper reminded her. Then the bell rang, and he rushed off to get his coffee.

So I was the only one left to see Imogen running her finger gently over the kitten in the picture on the cover, and muttering, 'Good!'

As if she were glad to hear it.

And as if it were news.

CHAPTER THREE

Was she more careful after that? I couldn't say. If you don't know exactly what you're looking for, you're often not sure what you've seen. She acted normally enough from then on. I heard her draw her breath in sharply once or twice. But the top shelf is pretty high, and it can be tiring, reaching up over and over to put things back after wet break.

But I was still curious about her and books. So whenever I came across one I really loved, I held it up.

'Have you read this?'

Sometimes she nodded. Sometimes she shook

her head. But she never burst out with the sort of
thing everyone else says.

'Oh yes! Didn't you just *love* the bit where his
head flipped off, and it turned out he was an
alien?'

Or, 'I *hated* the creepy old lady. I knew she was
out to get them from the very first page.'

Or even things like, 'Did you cry when the dog died? I cried *buckets*. My dad had to make me a cup of tea!'

No, she'd just put on that closed look people get when they're trying to get past charity collectors in the street, and try to fob me off.

'I think I read it, yes.'

'You must *remember*.'

She'd try and distract me. Even though hardly anyone had come near the book corner for days, she'd pretend we were so busy she had to interrupt to ask, 'Should this book here be put away? Or do I leave it out for the next project group?'

And I'd give up.

But, next day, when I held one of my favourites up to her face, I did quite definitely see her shudder.

'You have read this one, then? You know what it's about.'

'Well, *sort* of . . .'

'Didn't you get to finish it?'

19

She tossed her head vaguely. You couldn't tell if she meant yes, or no.

'Well, *did* you?'

She wouldn't answer. She just asked a question of her own. 'What did you want to say about it, anyway?'

'Nothing,' I muttered grumpily, and went back to my sorting. I had decided there was no point in trying to talk to Imogen about the books. I think, if two of you have read the same things, you should be able to have a good long chat about them, not have to put up with the other person ending each conversation by staring uncomfortably at her feet, and mumbling things like, 'Yes, I suppose so,' or, 'I'm not sure I remember that bit very well,' or, 'Maybe that wasn't actually the book I read.' I felt so cross about it, I even complained about her to Mr Hooper.

'Why have you dumped her on me? She's not much of a reader.'

He burst out laughing. 'Melly, compared with you, no-one in this class is a reader.'

I shook my head. 'No,' I said stubbornly. 'There's more to it than that. She says she's read things when she really hasn't.'

'Maybe you intimidate her,' he said. And then he added firmly, 'Just make an effort to be friendly, Mel. A week's not long. It won't hurt you.'

Seeing my face, he reached behind him to the

20

shelf, and tipped a big fat book out of a jiffy bag into my hands.

'There you are, Mel,' he said. 'Here's a reward for all your sufferings. And don't expect to be able to talk to Imogen about this one, because practically nobody else in the world has read it.'

'How do you know?'

'Because it's hot off the press,' he said proudly. 'A free gift from the publishers for ordering all those other books at the end of last term.'

I turned it over. *Red Rock*, by Alston Byers. The cover was a bit wet. A little girl in a blue frock was picking up stones. But some of the best books in the world have the worst covers, so I started it anyway, under the desk at the end of Maths Workbook.

It was amazing. I thought at first it was going to be one of those stories too stuffed with descriptions. It seemed to start with an awful lot of heat hazes lying over scrubland, and people leaning against the doors of sun-blistered shacks.

But suddenly it turned into a real nail-biter about a tribe of Indians who got fed up with tourists chipping off bits of their famous sacred red rock, to take home as souvenirs. So they put a curse on all the bits missing. Instantly, all over the world, reports started coming in of horrible deaths, and gruesome accidents, and weird diseases, as if some ghastly jump-in-your-seat horror video was playing everywhere, but, this time, for real.

I couldn't put the book down. Mr Hooper went through all his usual routines.

'Am I going to have to take that book off you till going home time, Melly?'

'I hope you're not rushing that written work to get back to your reading.'

'What's all this Mrs Springer tells me about you hiding that book I gave you under your song sheet?'

But it was impossible to stop reading. By this time in the story, people couldn't post back their bits of red rock fast enough. But one little girl, the one you can see on the cover, had slid a tiny chip into the pocket of her frock without her parents even noticing. It had fallen out into the suitcase. And there it lay, out of sight and out of mind, through all the dreadful things that had begun to happen to her family, one after another, because of the curse.

I had the usual problems that night at home, as well.

'I'm warning you, Melly. This light's going out in five minutes.'

'People your age still need their sleep, you know.'

'Why can't you just put it down, and finish it tomorrow?'

But finally, next morning, I reached the end. Gordon was desperate to have it next, so I made its card out right away, and during library hour I put *Red Rock* on top of the pile of books in front of Imogen.

'Can you stick a yellow dot on this one, so Gordon can take it home today?'

'Sure,' she said, reaching out for it. And then the blood drained from her face. It was extraordinary. I must have read the words a hundred times. *'Her cheeks went pale.' 'Her face went ashen.' 'She turned quite white with shock.'* But I would never in a thousand years have guessed it looked like this. It was as if someone had pulled a plug in the bottom of her feet.

I was sure she was fainting, so I stepped in close, to catch her as she fell. And that's the only reason I was near enough to hear her whispering to the little girl on the book cover.

'No! Not that bit of rock! Don't pick up that one, *please*!'

'Imogen?'

Startled, she looked up, her face still grey and clammy. 'What?'

She hadn't realized that I'd heard.

'Nothing,' I muttered. And it was true that, when it came to saying something, my mind had gone completely blank.

But I was thinking plenty. After all, she couldn't possibly have read the book.

So how could she have known what was going to happen?

Chapter Four

That's when I went to talk to Mr Hooper a second time. Don't get me wrong. I love ghost tales as much as anyone. I adore stories in which people have weird dreams, and strange things happen. But that's in books. Real life is supposed to be real, and I like my world to be solid around me. After all, nobody wants to find themselves suddenly trapped in the haunted house they've been watching on television, sensing a presence, and feeling the air going ice-cold around them.

But I was too spooked to go about it the right way. Instead of explaining properly, I just rushed up to Mr Hooper and asked him, 'Can I please dump Imogen now? She knows her way around, and everything.'

He wasn't pleased.

'Melly,' he said to me sternly. 'I've told you before, a week is only a week. Now try and be friendly. It'll be good for you.'

I felt like saying, 'You can talk. You were much nicer to Jason when he was new.' But he'd have thought I was just being cheeky, so I gave up and walked away. And since there was only one more day to go, I tried sticking it out. But it's not easy, sitting next to someone who sees through the covers into books. You can't ask straight out, 'Are you some sort of witch? Do you have second sight?' So I thought I was going about it in a pretty polite and roundabout way when, strolling back from the lunch hall, I said, all casually, 'Imogen, do you believe in looking into the future?'

She spun to face me. 'Looking into the future?'

'You know,' I said. 'Crystal balls and stuff. Knowing about things even before they happen.'

Now she was looking positively hunted. 'Why are you asking?' she demanded. 'Have people been talking about me?'

All the unease I'd been feeling curdled in the pit of my stomach. Either this new girl was a whole lot cleverer at teasing than I'd imagined, or the world was shifting nastily under my feet.

'Tell me you're joking, Imogen.'

You could see that she knew she'd made a big mistake.

'Of course I'm joking,' she tried to backtrack. 'I was just having you on.'

But I could feel hairs rising on the back of my neck, because I knew she was lying.

I looked around. Practically everyone in the class was in the school grounds with us. Why did it have to be *me*?

'Listen, Imogen,' I told her. 'You know that I was only asked to look after you for the first week, not stick like glue for life. And this is our last day, so I'll be taking off now, if that's all right with you.'

I'd have looked hurt, but she looked devastated.

'But, Melly. I thought we were—'

She stopped, and stared down at her feet while the word 'friends' echoed, unspoken, between us. She looked as if she'd been slapped. I couldn't try and pretend that everyone's first-week minder simply strides off halfway through the last day. And I hate lying. So it just popped out.

'I'm sorry, Imogen. I really am. But I can't be friends with you. You're just too *creepy*. I'm too *scared*.'

If someone blurted something like that out in my face, I'd stare in astonishment, and squawk, '*What?*' But Imogen simply looked as if she'd been half expecting it.

'All right,' she said, turning away. 'It doesn't matter.'

'You do understand?'

'Oh, yes,' she said. 'I understand.'

And somehow that made me feel a whole lot worse. Imagine how you'd feel if you refused to be friends with someone who's only ever been perfectly polite and anxious to please, just because they were different or had something wrong with them. And then imagine they said that to you.

Like me, you'd feel an absolute worm.

I stood and watched her walk away. She didn't look back. She didn't even try to pretend she had something to do in the cloakroom. She just set off towards the emptiest part of the school grounds, where she'd be alone. I dug my book out of my bag and turned the other way, to head for the lunchtime library.

And then I thought suddenly: 'Poor Imogen! Now she can't even go there.'

And I felt even *worse*. You see, all the way through school, I've used book corners and lunchtime library to hide away, and spend my break times reading. You know as well as I do that being a bookworm in school is like having a protective shield. It sends a message: 'Please leave me out of things unless I ask. Act as if I'm not here. It's not that I'm lonely. It's just that I'm happy on my own.'

And it is true. I wouldn't want to have to get through even one day the way the others do it. I see them, constantly in each other's company, always cheerful, always chatty. They never get ratty when someone suddenly begins to plait their hair without even asking, or begs to try on their glasses, or pesters them for hours about who is their favourite singer. Twenty different people can come up, one after another, and tell them something they already know, like, 'You've got a cold,' or, 'Those are new shoes you're wearing,' and they keep smiling. They don't even *mind*.

I don't know how they do it. I'd go mad. So making someone feel even a tiny bit awkward about hiding away anywhere, especially the book corner, would be, to me, like snatching away a lifebelt.

I couldn't do it to my own worst enemy. I certainly couldn't do it to someone who'd never done anything except try to be pleasant and helpful.

I had to run after her. 'Imogen! Wait a minute! Stop!'

And she turned and smiled at me. So that was that settled.

CHAPTER FIVE

It must have been a good long while since Imogen had had a friend. No-one else wanted to be near her. This was the reason, she admitted, she'd left her old school. Only a few of her classmates had gone around whispering that she was 'creepy' – the ones she thought must have been talking to me – but all of the rest had kept away from her as much as possible, making giant great fusses if they were even asked to share a desk or a table.

'What, even in work groups?'

The tears sprang. 'It was *horrible*.'

I felt so sorry for her. And the teachers had

found her crying in corners so often that, in the end, they had suggested she might be better starting afresh in a new school.

Ours.

The problem was, of course, that you could see it was all happening again, exactly the same. Everyone except me avoided her. It wasn't like giving someone the big freeze because they've been spiteful, or something. In fact, I don't believe people even realized they were doing it. But somehow, everywhere Imogen went, everyone melted away.

And it wasn't just the book corner, because the first time I really noticed it, she and I were walking down the corridor towards the lunch room. Paul had bent down to tie up his shoe-lace, but, as the two of us came close, I saw him hastily straighten up and drift off, with his shoe-lace flapping.

Funny, I thought.

And then the two girls from another class who had been sitting on the window-ledge, sharing a book, suddenly closed it without a word, and wandered away.

We went into lunch, and, now I'd noticed it, I realized it had been happening all week. Whenever the two of us had headed for a busy table, within seconds everyone was stacking their dishes back onto their trays, and taking them over to the hatches.

Then, on the way back from the cloakroom on my own, I bumped into Maria and Tasj.

'Don't you find it a bit creepy, going round with her?' Tasj asked me outright. 'She's so *weird.*'

'Seriously strange,' agreed Maria.

I tried to defend her. 'She doesn't bother me. I get on with her all right.'

But I was definitely the only one. It wasn't just Mr Hooper who avoided her. Even the other teachers seemed to move away when she was near. That afternoon I stood waiting while Imogen rooted in her book bag to make sure she still had her calculator. Just across the hall, Miss Harvey and Mr Sands were standing together, checking something on a chart. Suddenly, Mr Sands looked quite distracted. He glanced round uneasily, then said to Miss Harvey, 'Shall we go and do this—' He obviously couldn't think of anywhere else they should be doing it, so he just finished up lamely, '—somewhere else?'

I didn't think the idea would go down very well. Miss Harvey's famous in our school for not wasting time. She's usually telling the people in her class what to do even before she walks through the door. But now she, too, was looking round a bit uncomfortably, a bit unsure. And together, still holding the chart, they moved off across the hallway.

Away from their classrooms, I noticed.

Away from Imogen.

And away from me.

So even I ended up having to ask myself how I could stand being so close to someone so spooky. And I can't really explain, except to say that, from the moment I ran after her, she never bothered me at all the way she bothered other people. I never felt the urge to drift away. Now, looking back, I wonder if it was because I was the only one who knew for certain there was something strange about her. I didn't have to share their vague, uneasy feeling. But sometimes I think that all that time spent with my head in books had made weird people so familiar to me that I barely thought twice. After all, no-one writes a story that boils down to, 'Once, there was a normal young girl, and nothing of interest happened her whole life.' And, if they did, no-one would bother to read it. Would you have finished the last book you read if it had been about a plain, happy person doing nothing but plain, happy things?

When you were three, perhaps. Certainly not now.

So I was interested in her. And she turned out to be the perfect friend for someone like me. She was quiet, and she didn't mind spending half her life in the book corner and the other half in the library.

But, though he didn't seem to want to spend too much time near her himself, the fact that she didn't mix with the others did bother Mr Hooper.

'Imogen, maybe you shouldn't be spending all your time skulking between bookshelves like Melly.'

I looked up from the thriller I was reading. 'This is a school,' I teased him. 'You ought to be pleased we're sitting quietly with our noses in books.'

And he never noticed that, though my nose was, hers certainly wasn't. It even took me a while to realize that Imogen never actually read a book. Oh, she'd run her fingertips along the shelves, and pick one out. She had her favourites. One had a country scene on the cover.

"It was so pretty it could have been made of gingerbread..."

Another had children playing happily with puppies and kittens.

"But, best of all, Flora loved Little Fluffy."

She'd settle on one of the little yellow tubs, hold the book in her lap and stare off in the distance. If someone walked past, she'd open what she'd chosen quickly, anywhere, and look down until they'd gone by.

But most of the time she was just sitting with a look of pure enchantment on her face, as if she'd been whisked away somewhere magical.

'Happy?' I'd ask her, and she'd nod dreamily.

Then, 'Happy?' she'd ask me back, and I'd nod as well, because things were going pretty well for me, too, now that Mr Hooper had at last got me down for having a friend, and stopped nagging me about mixing and joining in, and all that stuff.

Yet Imogen kept everyone away.

Especially in swimming. And I love swimming. It's the only sport I like. Mr Hooper says that's because it's practically the only thing we do in school in which I know I'm safe from hearing things like, 'Now get yourselves into two teams,' or 'Choose groups to work in,' or the one that I really loathe, which is, 'Now choose a partner.'

And it is true, I love that feeling when you've finally found a bit of a space in the middle of all that shrieking and splashing. You let your feet slip out in front of you along the tiles, your head slides under, your hair floats up like weed, and just for a moment everyone's vanished. It's just you and your own magical, glistening bubbles.

Then someone steams past, kicking and shrieking, and the world's back again, spoiling it totally.

But Imogen worked like a secret barrier. Nobody except me realized, but from the moment she began picking her way down the steps into the shallows, everyone else was suddenly deciding to practise their racing starts up at the deep end of the pool, or hang by their feet from the bar along the other side.

It was brilliant for me. If I stayed near her, there was so much clear space around us that I could even practise my tumble turns.

'Keep on like this,' said Miss Rorty, 'and you'll win that Harries Cup for sure. I'll put my money on you.'

Over and over I pushed myself back from the side, to try again. And it was only after she blew the whistle, and I was getting out, that I had that really chilling thought.

Miss Rorty was horrified. 'Look at you, child!' she said, snatching up the nearest towel, and wrapping me tight, as if I were one of the infants. 'You're covered in goose-pimples. You're shivering fit to burst!'

But it wasn't cold. I didn't want to explain it, even if I could have done, through chattering teeth. It was something quite different.

The thought had suddenly struck me, getting out, that it was all very well for me to think that there was something weird about Imogen. But what about me?

After all, what would *you* think? How would *you* explain someone not even minding spending half an hour in a corner of the pool which, if they thought about it for a moment, they would have to admit was practically halfway to being haunted?

40

Chapter Six

Then she came top in something. It was *terrifying*. We'd just finished reading *Tyke Samuel* together as our book in class. 'Now write an essay,' Mr Hooper said. 'Pretend you're little orphan Sam, sent up to clear the chimneys of some great house. Write what he's thinking.'

I love it when Mr Hooper doesn't spoil things by making us talk about our stories before we write them. I settled down at once, and scribbled frantically till the bell rang. I didn't look up much, but, when I did, I saw that instead of staring round the room as usual, sucking her pencil, Imogen was busily writing, too.

Mr Hooper made Tasj collect them all for him at the end, finished or not, and then we rushed out, because it was going home time. But when we came back in the morning, he was looking thrilled.

'I'm pleased with everyone. Most of you did a good job. But one of the stories was astonishing. Truly outstanding.'

I know it sounds as if I'm being Mrs Boastie. But I did really think it must be me.

'Imogen!'

I wasn't the only person to turn and stare. (We all knew how awful her work was.) But no-one could doubt that she'd written every word of it all by herself, because we'd been in the room with her.

Mr Hooper handed her sheets of paper back. 'Go on. Read it out to everyone.'

She fingered her necklace anxiously. 'Oh, no! I couldn't.'

'Of course you can.'

'No, really!'

But Mr Hooper can't stand what he calls 'people being silly'. 'Imogen,' he said in his firm voice. 'Just stop fussing, and read it out to everyone now.'

Her fingers trembled as she held it up in front of her. The pages shook. She started off in such a nervous, stumbling voice that we couldn't make sense of it. She was tripping over some words. She was puzzling over others. You'd think, to watch and listen, she'd never heard a word of it before, let alone written it.

In the end, Mr Hooper had to take pity on her. Stretching towards her, he prised the sheets of paper out of her hands, and went back to his own desk.

There, sitting on the desk, he read it properly.

It made my blood run cold. It was as if Tyke Sam was in the room with us, telling us everything. We sat like mice as he told of his terror of the dark, and how soot fell in showers, blinding him, blocking his ears, and even filling his mouth if he'd been rash enough to open it to gasp, or take a breath between his sobs.

'And once,' he told us, '*I tumbled down the shaft of a chimney into an unswept grate and sent a lady into a fit of screams. I thought I'd startled her out of her wits, because she began to shriek, "Chimney rat! Chimney rat!" over and over.*

'*But then I realized it was the flying soot that had put her in a fury. And the woman beside her tugged me out from where I crouched, scraped*

and bleeding, behind the big brass firescreen, and boxed my poor ears till they rang.'

Everyone shivered. 'They couldn't do that, could they?' Bridie asked. But Mr Hooper didn't answer her. He just read on.

'I have this fear that grips me. I think I'm going to stick fast so high up that they can't hear my cries. I think they'll wait a day or so. And then *decide, for their convenience, it's easier to think that I'm already dead, because it's chilly and they want a fire.'*

That was when Imogen jumped to her feet, and ran from the classroom, holding her hands over her ears.

We all stared at the door she'd left wide open. 'That is so *weird*,' said Bridie. 'If she can *write* something as scary and horrible as that, how come she can't sit and listen when it's read aloud?'

'Perhaps it embarrassed her,' said Mr Hooper. But I knew better. And when he sent me after her, to fetch her back, I told her so.

'That wasn't your story at all, was it? It was still Tyke Sam's.'

She looked up from the cloakroom bench, and snapped defiantly, 'Don't be ridiculous!'

But she'd understood what I meant at once, I noticed. So I persisted. 'It's true, isn't it? You left your hand on the book as you were writing, and he poured his story out through you.'

'That is the silliest—'

'Listen,' I interrupted, pushing Stephen's football gear to the side, and sitting beside her. 'I'm not trying to be rude, but someone like you could no more write a story like that than fly to the moon.'

'I could!'

'No, you couldn't. I know. I sit next to you, remember? *And* I've been watching you.'

The colour crept up, past the gold necklace and up to her cheeks. 'There's nothing to watch!'

'Oh, yes, there is. You're very strange, you know. Everyone senses it. But I think I'm the only one who's begun to fit it together. I think you can see into books. For you, books aren't just imaginary worlds. They're real. Real people, in real places.'

She was still trying to fight back. 'I don't know what you're—'

'Imogen!' I was getting impatient. 'I've guessed your secret. Can't you see? You might as well give up, and tell me all about it. Because you can't just keep on rushing out of classrooms, and changing schools, and finding it so hard to concentrate that all the work you do is rubbish unless some character in a book is writing it for you.'

Her eyes filled up with tears. 'That's *horrible*.'

'It might be horrible, but it's *true*.'

I knew I was winning. 'Listen,' I said to her gently. 'You know you can't carry on like this. You have to talk to somebody. And you can trust me.'

The tears spilled over. She rooted in her pocket to find a tissue, and I sat waiting.

In the end, she turned towards me and looked hard, as if she were working something important out. As if she were *inspecting* me.

And then, suddenly, her face cleared. It was as if the sun had come out inside her. She looked a different person.

'Yes,' she said. 'I think you're right. I think that I can trust you. After all, I'm not the only one who's different. You're different, too, in your own way. What's odd about you is that you're not so tied up with all the others that you have to share secrets. I really do think you could treat it all like just another story in one of your precious books, that you can close when you want. So I can tell you.'

'Right,' I said. 'Story-time. After lunch in the book corner. Deal?'

And Imogen smiled.

'Yes,' she said. 'Deal. After lunch, I'll tell you the story.'

CHAPTER SEVEN

If it were a book, I couldn't put it down, I'll tell you that. I'd find it a real keep-you-upper. Once she had started, out it poured in torrents. How it began when she was tiny, before she could even read. She had been helping her cousin take down the decorations after Christmas, and he was teasing her.

'The youngest person in the house has to wear everything off the tree for a whole week.'

She was so innocent that she believed him. So she stood still while Eddie hooked all of the glittering ornaments off the tree onto her woolly. He draped the tinsel round her, and then, as if she weren't already looking sparkly enough, added a few chocolate Santas and some glitter stars, and then all the rings and bracelets and necklaces he could find in their granny's old jewellery box.

By the time Imogen's mother walked in with the post, there wasn't an inch of herself, said Imogen, that wasn't twinkling or flashing or jangling.

'Aren't you the Sparkling Lady!' her mother had said admiringly, dropping the letters on the table, and opening the first packet. Then, 'Well, that's very quick. It's the Christmas snaps, back already.'

Shedding ornaments over the carpet, Imogen rushed to look. Eddie took the top one. 'Look at Aunt Beth, asleep with her mouth open!'

Imogen fanned the photographs over the table, and giggled at Uncle Ted in his paper hat. Then she said sadly, 'No Aunty Dora.'

Her mother pointed at the photographs. 'Yes, she's there, sweetheart. Under your finger. And here. And sitting next to the tree in this one.'

But Imogen still looked forlorn, and said again, 'No. No Aunty Dora.'

Now her cousin was getting impatient. 'Don't be silly, Immy.' He stabbed at the photos with his finger. 'She's in this one. And this one.'

Imogen's woolly jangled as she tossed her head. 'Aunty Dora's gone.'

'Gone where, sweetheart?'

But there was no way Imogen could explain. And her mother had stopped trying to listen even before the phone rang with the terrible news.

'That's awful,' I said. 'So did your mother guess?'

'Not then,' said Imogen. 'It was only when it happened a second time, ages later, that she thought back and remembered that morning with the Christmas photos.'

'Why? Was the second time the same sort of thing?'

52

'No. It was different. But it was just as *strange*. I'd had a horrible day. I'd lost the toss in my ballet class, and couldn't be the princess in the show.' She grinned, embarrassed. 'I came home in *floods*. Mum did her best. "You be a princess for *me*," she said. So I dressed up and started dancing. But it was stupid, so I ended up in tears again. Mum pulled me onto her lap, and read me a story about a little pit pony called Patch. And suddenly I was going mad, struggling and screaming about water closing over Patch's head. And when we got further into the story—'

'I know,' I told her. 'I had that book, too. That's a horrible bit, when he falls in the water.'

"And it seemed to poor Patch that he would never again reach firm ground..."

Imogen shivered. 'Well, next day, when I was calm again, and we reached that part in the story, Mum stopped and gave me a funny look. "You knew this, didn't you?" And that's when she guessed.'

'My mum would just have thought I'd had the book read to me in school.'

'I think mine would have thought that, except that she says she's always had a bit of a gift that way herself.'

'I'm not sure why she'd call it a "gift",' I said.

Imogen looked blank.

I tried to explain. 'I don't mean to be rude, but most of the time your work is *terrible*, and half of the books in the school give you the frights. On top of that, it seems that if you don't watch out where you're putting your fingers, you know in advance when terrible things are going to happen – in books *and* in real life.' I spread my hands. 'Hardly a gift,' I continued. 'More like some sort of *blight*.'

From the look on her face you'd have thought that I'd said she had some mangy disease, or something. She looked so upset I had to change the subject quickly.

'So how does it work, then, this strange gift of yours?'

'Work?' The question puzzled her a little. 'Well, it's a sort of imagining. Like in a dream.'

'What sort of dream?'

'Depends. If the book that I'm touching is happy, then it's lovely. Like being there, but on a cloud. In things, but not quite.'

'Like reading,' I said. 'Like being lost in a book.'

'*More*,' she insisted. And I remembered all the times I'd seen her sitting lost in a rapturous world of her own.

'How?' I asked. 'I mean, suppose you were holding *Tansy at St Clare's*?'

'You might dream the midnight feast bit. You'd smell the cakes, and feel a part of the chatter around you.

"'We'll do it eeny meeny miny mo,' said Laura..."

'Or if it was *Philippa and the Midnight Pony*, you'd feel the cold air on your face, the hooves thudding beneath you, and all the excitement.'

Then I remembered all the times she'd acted as if she'd practically been bitten.

'So what if it's a chiller thriller, or a horror book?'

'Oh, then it's *awful*, like being trapped in a nightmare. You have all these horrible and panicky feelings as you see every ghastly thing about to happen, like a train coming round the bend while the car's still stuck on the crossing, or the toddler leaning too far out of the top-floor window. But, just like in a bad dream, there's nothing you can do to help. You just have to stand there, holding your breath, and watching and waiting.'

'You can't *ever* stop it?'

'No. Because it's already there, in the words on the page.'

I thought for a bit. Then I said, 'You take that book, *Clown Colin*—'

She waved her hands frantically in front of her face. 'No! Don't! I hate even thinking about when his wooden eyes start spinning round and round. Don't even talk about it!'

I tried another one. 'How about *Little Mattie*?'

'Noo-oo!' she wailed. 'That bit where he's dragged away from his mum – I can't *bear* it!'

"...until he couldn't even see her any more."

That is so *weird*, I thought. And I couldn't have felt more sorry for her. After all, I read more than my fair share of books that make me keep the light on all night long. And lots of books that make me sad, or anxious, till things work out right. But I don't end up in a state like her, halfway to fainting because of three or four grisly pages, and not even able to look at the cover of that book ever again without wanting to shudder.

'A gift', her mother called it. But, the more Imogen told me about it, the more I thought that that was totally the wrong word.

'Curse' was more like it.

Yes. Not 'gift', but 'curse'.

CHAPTER EIGHT

I had a hundred more questions, but the bell had rung, and when we got back to the classroom, Mr Hooper was in one of his 'Time-to-start-something-new' moods.

'*Compare and Contrast*,' he announced. And through the long afternoon we tried it with fifty different things: light and dark, noise and silence, misery and happiness, on and on and on.

'And that's your homework,' he told us afterwards. 'One and a half pages of Compare and Contrast.'

'Can we do anything?' I asked him.

'Anything.'

'And can it be private?'

'I suppose so.'

(For 'Private', you put a large red P up in the top corner. Then, even if it's the best piece of work in the class, he won't read it out to everyone.)

I had a plan. As we left class, I said to Imogen, 'Shall I walk home with you? I'll come as far as your house, and then cut back through Stannard's car park.'

She seemed so pleased, I felt a little guilty. And I felt worse when Mr Hooper, who'd been listening, whispered in my ear, 'See? Wasn't I right? Once you get used to it, it's nice to have company.'

But even knowing I was using her to do my homework didn't stop me asking her questions all the way back to her house.

'Was your mum pleased when she realized you could see into books and photos? Or was she horrified?'

'She was excited,' Imogen admitted. 'I think people always teased her when she said she knew things were going to happen. So I think she was pleased I took after her a little bit.'

'Does she encourage it?'

'Encourage it?'

I tried to explain. 'When my mum realized I was good at swimming, she signed me up at swim club right away. But when she found out I could crack my fingers, she couldn't stop me fast enough. "Don't do that!" she kept saying. "It's a horrible habit!"'

Imogen considered. 'But this isn't like either of those things. It just happens, or it doesn't.'

'Is that what your mum thinks?'

'I suppose so.'

'So she doesn't go round shoving books at you, just out of curiosity, to see what happens?'

'Of course she doesn't.'

'But she hasn't done anything to put a stop to it, either?'

Imogen stared. 'Like *what*?'

I couldn't think of anything, anyhow. Somehow, when it came down to it, it hardly seemed polite to mention going to doctors, or hypnotists, or psychiatrists, or anything like that. And anyhow, maybe Imogen and her mother were right, and being able to see into books and photos was one of those things, like blue eyes or freckles, that you couldn't do anything about if you wanted.

So I just kept on with the questions, ticking the answers off in my head, ready for later.

'Well, does it worry her that it's so hard for you to concentrate on your schoolwork?'

'I try not to say too much about that,' Imogen admitted.

'But she must know you're having problems.

What about when you had to change schools because people thought you were—' I would have said 'creepy', but it seemed nicer to finish up '– a little *strange*?'

'She was surprised it all got so difficult so quickly.'

'Did it?'

'Oh, yes. Before last year, it only ever happened those two times – with Aunty Dora's photo, and that book about the pony. I still had plenty of friends. And my work wasn't bad, either.'

That made sense. After all, she'd written out that story from Tyke Sam pretty fast, covering three whole pages in less than half an hour. And Mr Hooper could read it.

'So this whole business just got worse suddenly?'

'Yes,' Imogen said. 'And maybe one day it'll go away again just as quickly.'

'Would you like that?'

She didn't answer. She just stared ahead.

'How about your mum?' I asked. 'Would *she* like it?'

'Why are you asking all these questions?' Imogen burst out.

I shut up, fast, in case she guessed. But anyway, we were already turning the corner into her road. Imogen led me past three or four plain, boring old houses, then up the path beside another, just the same.

'Mum's probably round the back,' she said, pushing open the side gate. I followed her through, and stopped in my tracks, astonished. The back of the house was amazing. I just *stared*.

How to describe it? It looked as if fairies and goblins had decorated the whole place for a joke. The bricks were yellow, the door red, the window frames green and their shutters blue. All over the lawn were tiny pretend windmills, and gnomes fishing in ponds, and plaster tortoises and rabbits. There was even a wizard sitting cross-legged on a stone mushroom, waving his wand. If you were five, you would have thought you'd fallen

through a hole in the real world, and ended up in
a Toytown picture book.

'That is incredible!'

Behind me, there was an excited voice. 'Do you really like it? *Really?*'

I spun round.

'Melly,' said Imogen. 'This is my mum.'

She didn't look like anybody's mum to me. She was so *young*, and tall and bright-eyed, with blazing red hair tumbling over her shoulders like lava spilling out of a volcano. She wore a bright shawl, embroidered with sparkling butterflies, and when she reached out to fold her arms tightly round Imogen, to hug her, Imogen practically vanished beneath the butterflies and the waterfall of hair.

'Good day, my precious?'

I don't know what I was expecting Imogen to say. Maybe if I had someone from school standing there listening, I wouldn't start by launching into a great long wail about what Tyke Sam made me write being so horrid I had to leave the classroom.

But still I wouldn't have answered, like she did, 'It was lovely, Mum. Really good.' And sounded as if I meant it. I didn't know if it was because of me that she said nothing, or if she was putting a brave face on her horrible day to hide from her mother the fact that she'd cracked, and told her secret to someone outside the family.

But, whichever it was, her mother believed her. Her bright eyes twinkled happily. She tossed her hair back, and, releasing poor Imogen from her grasp, held her at arm's length like a toddler, peered in her eyes, and asked hopefully,

'And did anything "special" happen?'

I stared. My mum asks, 'Anything special happen?' But she's not really paying attention. If I answered, 'Yes, Mr Hooper fell off the roof and broke his neck,' she'd stop clattering pans around long enough to listen. And if I said, 'Yes, everyone teased me till I cried,' she'd be on the phone to Mrs Trent in a flash. But mostly, she asks casually. She's only checking. If something really interesting or funny happened, she wants to hear about it. But that's all.

But this was different. Imogen's mother's 'Anything "special" happen?' was clearly code for their little shared secret. I waited for Imogen to tell her. But she just shook her head.

And Mrs Tate looked really disappointed.

'Well, never mind,' she said, in that exact same tone Miss Rorty uses when I don't make my best time in the pool. 'Never mind.' She turned to me, and her face brightened. 'A visitor! How lovely!' She clapped her hands like someone in a pantomime. 'We must have iced cakes and home-made lemonade!'

'I really ought to be pushing off home now,' I told her. 'My mum will be—'

But she'd danced off. I mean it. She was literally dancing up the garden path, flapping her shawl like a giant great butterfly. I glanced across at Imogen, but she clearly hadn't even noticed I thought her mother was a little odd. And I can understand that. After all, if she came round to our house unexpectedly, and caught my mum all ratty and irritable because she's worried about money, or about Granny going back into hospital, she'd probably think our house was strange, and I wouldn't notice.

But there was certainly nothing ratty about Mrs Tate. Having tea with her and Imogen was like stepping into one of those old books you sometimes find in charity shops, with thick spongy paper and coloured illustrations hidden under tissue. Everything was 'thrilling', or 'perfectly wonderful', or 'absolutely scrumptious', or 'such, such fun!'

I couldn't wait to get away, back to my own mum.

She wasn't too pleased with me. 'Next time you're going to be an hour late, don't just leave a message to *tell* me. Ask me the day *before*.'

'I'm sorry,' I said, and rushed into some story about Imogen really needing someone to walk her home. But it was still a good half-hour before she'd calmed down enough for me to get on with this homework I was planning.

'What would you do if you found I could see into books?'

'See into books?'

'And photos.'

Mum's used to weird questions from me, depending on what I'm reading. But you could tell that this one baffled her.

'What do you mean?'

'Well,' I explained. 'Suppose each time I touched a book, I knew exactly what was in it.'

She gave a little snort of amusement. 'Now wouldn't your teachers all be pleased with that!'

'But it felt real. And sometimes it upset me.'

'Like when you read that ghastly book about that badger?'

'Much worse than that.'

Mum gave me a look. We both remembered what I was like, reading that badger book. She kept on trying to tug it away, but I kept snatching it back because, once I'd got started, I had to know what happened. But I couldn't stop crying, right through to the horrible end. And the minute I'd finished, Mum stuffed it in the dustbin.

*"And every leaf that rustled seemed to
shriek 'Danger!'"*

'Well,' she said thoughtfully. 'If it was going to be worse than that, I couldn't be doing with it.'

'What about the photos? Suppose I could tell how everyone in a photo was going to end up?'

'You mean, look at a school photograph, and be able to tell who'd end up in jail, and who'd end up prime minister?'

'That sort of thing.'

She shuddered. 'I can't imagine anything worse than being able to see into the future.'

'You wouldn't call it a gift, then?'

'No, I certainly wouldn't. It sounds terrible.'

'And you wouldn't encourage it?'

'*Encourage* it? I think I'd forbid it!'

'You can't forbid magic,' I reminded her.

'Oh, *can't* you?' said my mum, in such a determined '*I* could' tone of voice that I was practically assured on the spot that, if I'd been unlucky enough to be born with a gift like Imogen's, my mother would have splatted it flat in my cradle.

CHAPTER NINE

I was called up to the desk about my homework. Mr Hooper swung round in his chair till we both had our backs to everyone.

'Is this your idea of being a *friend*?' he asked me crossly, flapping my 'Compare and Contrast' work under my nose.

'I told you it was private,' I said stubbornly. 'And I put on a giant *P*.'

'Melly, this piece is *horrible*.'

'It's *true*,' I argued.

'But you can't write things just because they're *true*.'

'That's the whole *point* of writing,' I explained.

'Books say they're made up, but they're actually a lot more truthful than real life.'

'What do you mean?'

'Well, look,' I said. 'People feel *safer* if it's in a book. You can read about the most terrible people, and hardly think twice about it. But if you hear something even a quarter as bad about someone you know in real life, everyone goes bananas.' I pointed at my homework. 'See?'

That shut him up.

'*And*,' I went on, 'you know what's going on better in books.' I pointed over at Imogen. 'I'd have a whole lot better idea of what was going on in her house, and inside her head, if she were in a book. At least the person who wrote it wouldn't be too polite to tell me. As it is, I just have to *guess*.'

'Melly,' he told me sternly, 'I didn't try and help you make a friend just so you could start being nosy about her private life.'

'I thought people were supposed to be interested in their friends.'

'Interested, yes. Nosy, certainly not.'

'I don't see any difference.'

He couldn't explain it, that was obvious. He flicked the pages I'd written between his fingers once or twice, staring at me anxiously, while I thought how *useful* it would be to have an author around all the time to explain people properly, without all that stuff that everyone knows is not true really but feels they ought to say to be polite, like, 'Oh, I'm sure she didn't *mean* it', or, 'I expect she just forgot, dear', or, 'No, she likes you *really*'. Authors are braver, and more honest. They would explain why Imogen's mother was too wrapped up in planting silly joke gardens and thinking everything was fun and jolly, even to notice her daughter was being driven crazy because she'd had such a horrible gift passed on to her.

A gift passed on . . .

'Mel?' Mr Hooper was still staring at me.

'Sorry,' I said hastily. But still the words snagged in my brain. 'A gift passed on . . .' They were reminding me of something, but I couldn't think what.

Now Mr Hooper was sighing. 'You just don't get it, do you, Mel?'

'No.' I was getting irritable myself now. 'And I

don't think it's fair, you ticking me off like this. You said, "Compare and Contrast". You said we could do anything. And you agreed it could be private. I haven't shown my work to Imogen. I haven't hurt her feelings. I just chose something interesting, thought about it hard, and wrote it properly.'

'But, really, Mel! To write a piece about how your two mums are so different!' He peered at the top page in his hand. "*My mum might be horribly ratty, but at least she has a grip. You can depend on her.*" And fancy writing—' Again, he searched the page for the bit that had upset him. "*It must be awful having Mrs Tate as a mother. She might be the sort of person who can make a wet picnic fun, or giggle about anything. But you couldn't come to her with a problem. She'd just pretend it wasn't there, or didn't matter.*"'

'She would, too,' I insisted. 'Maybe you haven't met her, but I have.'

He slid the paper-clip off my pages, and folded them over and over till they were small enough to fit in his trouser pocket.

'This isn't going in your folder,' he said. 'I'm burning it. I'm not going to run the risk of Imogen ever seeing it.'

'Fine by me.'

'And you're to promise me you'll never mention it.'

'I promise.'

'Cross your heart?'

'Cross my heart.'

He gave me a good long look, and you could tell that what he really wanted to say was, 'Mel, you're so *weird*.' But he controlled himself.

'Right,' he said, swivelling back to face the rest of the class. 'This discussion is over.'

'Except—' I reminded him.

'Except?'

'My mark,' I said. 'You haven't told me what I got for it.'

Back came the stern look. 'Melly,' he said, 'I wouldn't mark this if you paid me my weight in gold.'

'But, if you *did* . . .?' I persisted.

He rolled his eyes. 'Mel, you're *incorrigible*.'

'Just tell me,' I begged. 'After all, I spent a good long time on it, and did it as well as I could.'

'Oh, very well!' he snapped. 'Since you have promised you'll never mention it again, I'll tell you what you would have got for it.'

I waited, knowing. And I was dead right.

Ten out of ten. Perfect *A*. Excellent!

Goody.

CHAPTER TEN

That afternoon, Imogen ended up in tears again. Our class was picking teams for indoor games. Arinda and Luke were calling.

'Tom.'

'Matty.'

'Pats. No! Sorry, I've changed my mind. Louay!'

'Then I'll have Pats.'

As I expected, Imogen was left even till after me. But, at the end, when he was still one person down, Luke turned away and started making plans. 'Who wants to be shooter?'

Me? I'd have been delighted if it happened. By the time Mrs Tallentire came back with the team sashes and ball, I'd have been tucked in the gap under the gym stairs, quietly reading. And if she was cross with me, I'd have been ready to argue. 'Well, what was I *supposed* to do? Nobody picked me.'

But Imogen stood there, drooping. ('Like a lily in a flood', as Mr Hooper calls it.) Her eyes were bright with tears. No-one in our class is positively spiteful. It was the old 'drift-away' business working again. Nobody else even noticed, not even Mrs Tallentire, who hardly gave Imogen a glance, let alone one of the sashes. So she did end up on our team, but on the very edge, along the wall, and I don't think the ball was thrown in her direction once, for the whole game.

'That's it!' I told her, after. 'Tomorrow, after school, we're off to the library.'

'The town library? Why?'

'You'll see.'

She kept up the pestering, but I wouldn't tell, in case she wouldn't come. Next day, we walked straight up the stairs to *Reference*, and still she hadn't guessed why we were there. I left her staring at the huge Map of World Animals while I got started.

Magic. *Superstitions*. *Legends*. If you don't believe them, then they're fascinating. I've sat for hours hunched over tales of banshees wailing to warn of deaths on the way, and soldiers who had died in a field hospital along the line scaring the wits out of their fellow officers by turning up on the dawn watch.

But if, like me, you have begun to think you're practically living in one of these stories, you're looking for something different. And it wasn't there. I ran my eyes down list after list on the computer screen, and scoured shelf after shelf. There were whole books on tarot cards and palm-reading, half a bookcase on haunted houses, tomes on black magic and spell-making, lots about poltergeists, even a pamphlet on spirit-writing.

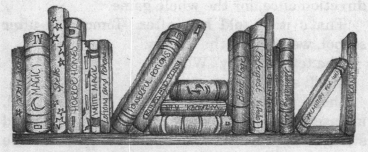

But nothing at all about giving it up.

Imogen wasn't helping. 'Look, Melly,' she kept saying. 'This isn't your problem. Stop worrying about me. I'm perfectly happy with things the way they are.'

'Oh, yes?'

'Yes.' She made a face. 'I know it's all sometimes a little bit upsetting—'

'A little bit *upsetting*?' I stared down from where I was balancing on one of the stumpy little library ladders. 'You practically *fall* into the most upsetting books. You even know when members of your family are coasting towards accidents. Everyone avoids you, and you can't even get on with your work. And you call that "a little bit upsetting"? Well, you must have nerves of steel.'

'All right!' she flared. 'Sometimes it's horrible, and I can't sleep at nights. But I still can't see what you're hoping to find in all these books.'

I reached up higher, to pull a couple of books without titles on their spines off the top shelf. 'Listen, Imogen. There has to be some way you can get out of this.'

'Get out of it?'

'Lose this "gift" of yours. Turn back into a normal person.'

'I *am* a normal person!'

'You know what I mean. And if your mum's right, and what you've got is like blue eyes, or curly hair, then you can't be the first.'

'So what are you looking for?'

'A book,' I said. 'I'll know it when I find it. It'll be something that explains what all the people who were like you before did to get rid of it.'

She looked quite blank.

'Listen,' I told her patiently. 'You don't think you're the first of your sort to be unpopular, do you? I'm sure seeing into the future has never been the best way of making and keeping friends. Don't tell me all those early soothsayers were daft enough to stroll around turning ashen every five minutes, and pointing at the next person who was going to fall down the well, because I don't believe it. The rest of the villagers would have stood for it only once or twice, and then drowned them in the duckpond.'

Imogen was silent. I do believe it must have been the very first time she'd given a thought to all the people who'd had the gift in centuries before. But that's one of the things you get from reading all the time – a sense of other places, other times, and other ways of doing things.

'So what are you telling me?' she asked at last.

'I'm not telling you anything,' I said, 'because I don't yet know. But you can be pretty sure that, whatever it is you want to find out about, somebody wanted to know it before you. And books have been invented for over four hundred years. So there's usually one about it somewhere.'

Again, I reached up to the very top shelf, this time for a volume called *Magical Thinking* which had caught my attention.

'My bet', I told her, 'is that most of these special people must have had the sense to lose this so-called "gift" of theirs as fast as they could. And I'm going to find out how they did it.'

'I bet they didn't *all* want to lose it,' she said stubbornly. 'I bet some of them thought that it was *interesting*.'

'Or *fun*,' I said scathingly. 'People like your mother.'

I heard the sharp intake of breath. But, struggling with my balance on the top step, I must have missed the sound of footsteps, and the swing doors closing behind her.

That, or another of her skills was Levitation. Or even Vanishing. Because, when I looked round again, she had gone.

CHAPTER ELEVEN

When someone does that to you, you're not quite sure if they've stormed off for good, or if they're going to show up again in a few minutes, pretending they just went off to buy sweeties or gum.

So I sat on the ladder a little while, hoping she'd reappear and flicking through *Magical Thinking* by Prof. J. B. Blackstaffe. It was a bit of a surprise, that book. You'd think someone like me, who reads so much, would have got used to the fact that titles so often turn out to mean something quite different from what you imagined when you first saw them on the shelf. I would have thought that *Magical Thinking* would be about spells, or the power of thought, or voodoo, or something.

In fact, it was poor old Professor Blackstaffe trying to persuade us to use our brains.

He posed little problems at the top of each page, and asked you questions. Then he told you what the Great Thinkers of the Past would have thought about each one.

While I was waiting for Imogen, I read the first.

> *Your good friend is wasting time in terrible company. One day, the wastrels move, and ask you to pass on their new address and phone number.*
>> *Do you:*
>>> *A: Refuse to accept the task?*
>>> *B: Take the details, rip them up, and say nothing?*
>>> *C: Pass the information on, with your usual warning?*

Most of the Great Thinkers of the Past turned out to be Stellar Fusspots, too, if you want my opinion. They mostly went for *A* or *C*. (I'd have picked *B*.) But when it was obvious Imogen wasn't coming, I gave up and put the book back on the shelf, and went on home.

I hoped by morning she'd have forgiven me for being so rude about her mother. But when I took my place beside her in the class, she turned away.

I tapped her shoulder. 'Look,' I said. 'That was a horrible thing I said, and I'm really sorry. But I was only trying to help you.'

'*Help* me?' She glowered. 'You mean, *bully* me, don't you?'

I stared at her. 'Is that really what you think I've been doing?'

'Well, isn't it? Dragging me off to the library when you can't find exactly what you want here in school? Making me hang around while you peer into every single book?'

'I'm only trying to find something that has to be there.'

Her eyes flashed. 'Oh, yes! It has to be there, of course! You know! And that's the trouble with you, Melanie Palmer. You think you know *everything*. But it doesn't even seem to have sunk into your big, fat, book-swollen brain that in that library there were about a billion books about harnessing the ancient mysteries, but none at all about giving it up!'

And she was rumbled. I had rumbled her. It's *words*, you see. Miss Rorty knows the spin on a ball. Mum senses when I'm coming down with something. Mr Hooper knows when someone's had too much help with their homework.

And I know words. I know exactly how they fit, and where they belong. I know who uses which ones, and I can always sense when they are out of place.

Or have been borrowed.

'"*Harnessing the ancient mysteries*"? Is that what your mother calls it?'

It was as if I'd pressed some button that said, '*Detonate!*' She went berserk. Tears spurted, and she flew at me, practically pushing me backwards off my chair.

'Shut up! My family's nothing to do with you! So just shut up!'

And don't we all know those words, too! Neil used to yell them all the time when his dad went to prison, and people in the classroom made even friendly remarks, or asked even reasonable questions. So now I at least had a clue to why Imogen kept secrets from her giddy, childlike mother, and hid the strains of all her days in school, and tried to keep pleasing with this horrible 'gift' of hers.

Like Neil, she was just trying to protect someone she loved who couldn't help but embarrass her.

And she had made enough noise doing it. Now everyone was staring. And when Mr Hooper came in through the door a moment later, his eyebrows were already raised. He must have heard from outside in the corridor.

I didn't want to make things worse for her. So I just tried to make a joke of it, moving my chair back and raising my arms, like someone protecting themselves from an attacker. But to her, I whispered, 'Sorry! I'm really sorry. I didn't mean to say anything nasty. I just thought it didn't sound like you. But I wasn't being rude about your mother again, honestly. In fact—'

If you'd seen her tearful face, you'd have lied too.

'In fact, I'm sure she's right. She knows an awful lot more than I do, after all, having a bit of a gift herself. I only dragged you to the library because I was *curious*.'

Mollified, Imogen stopped scowling so fiercely.

'Friends?' I asked tentatively.

There was a moment's silence, then, 'All right, then. Friends,' she agreed, a little unwillingly.

I didn't like to push it, so I was good as gold all day. Mr Hooper helped. Twice, he sent me off on good long jobs, to give us a rest from each other. But things were still a little prickly, so when she rather diffidently asked me if I wanted to walk home with her, I didn't like to tell her it was my swimming evening and I didn't have time, so I invited her along instead.

'We practically drive down your street. Mum won't mind stopping to pick you up.'

In fact, Mum was delighted. (Like Mr Hooper, she's always relieved to find I'm not completely allergic to spending time with real people.) So, even though you could tell that something about Imogen made her a bit uneasy, she was nice to her all the way, asking her how she was enjoying being in a new school, and whether she was getting along with Mr Hooper, and what she liked doing best – even trying to get Imogen into the pool as an extra on our Family Swimsaver Ticket.

While the man at the cash desk was reaching down our locker key bracelets, Imogen and I stood back against the wall. I pointed to one of the framed photographs opposite.

'That looks exactly like the Harries Cup.'

Imogen grinned. 'You really want to win it, don't you, Mel?'

'I've wanted it for *three years*,' I confessed. 'The first year, Toby Harrison beat me by a couple of metres. That was fair enough. Then, last year, Mum wouldn't even let me try.'

Imogen stared across at my mum. 'Wouldn't *let* you?'

'I did have flu,' I admitted. 'But still I'm sure I could have done it. There was only Phoebe Tucker in the running, and I was a good five seconds faster than her over the whole three lengths. But this year she's too old to enter. So,' I said, flattening myself back against the wall to let a man with a pushchair get past, 'in two weeks' time, Mr

Archibald Leroy, Councillor for Leisure Services, will be handing the Harries Cup to *me*.'

'No, he won't,' said Imogen.

'Sorry?'

I'd turned to stare at her, but just at that moment, Mum hurried over. 'What a time that took! Let's hope there's no more messing about, or it won't have been worth coming.' She held out her cupped hands. 'Right, then. Hand it all over. Money, watches, diamonds . . .'

She makes the same joke every week. I slid off my watch, and passed it across.

'And you, dear.' Mum turned to Imogen. 'What about that necklace?'

Imogen patted it. 'No, really. It's all right. I always swim in it. The clasp's so stiff it never comes undone by accident.'

'I'm not sure that's wise,' Mum said. 'It's one thing wearing it in a school lesson, when everyone knows it's yours. But this session is different.'

'All right.' Imogen turned her back to me. 'Can you get it undone, Mel?'

I struggled with the clasp. She was quite right, it was horribly stiff and difficult. But finally I managed to prise it open. The slim gold chain fell like a tiny living snake into my palm. It was so cold, it startled me. And though I was sure it was imagination, it seemed to stir of its own accord, even before I prodded it with my finger.

'What are those strange scratches on it?' Mum asked, opening her bag for me to spill the glittering loops of gold safely inside.

'My mother says they're charms,' said Imogen. 'The wavy shapes stand for water, and the pointy ones for roots.'

'Curious,' said Mum, snapping her bag shut. 'And much safer here with me than in those lockers.' She set off up the stairs for the café, and I turned to Imogen.

'Why did you *say* that?' I demanded.

'About the roots and water?'

'No,' I said. 'About Councillor Leroy not being there to give me the Harries Cup.'

'I didn't say that. All I said was—'

She stopped, and stared at me, appalled. I couldn't work out what was wrong with her. It wasn't quite like all the times before, when blood drained from her face. But she still looked horrified enough.

'Oh, no!' she whispered, her eyes on me, huge and round.

'What's up?' I asked her. 'Is it bad news about Councillor Leroy? Is he going to *die*?'

She shook her head and tried to pull herself together. But though she tried to answer sensibly, she still looked weird. Not scared, exactly. More sort of cagey. Shifty-looking, even.

'What's going on?' I demanded. 'Imogen, what's going on?'

She took a breath and said firmly: 'Nothing. Nothing at all.' But she was still looking hunted, and, desperate to distract me, she glanced around.

'Oh, look!' She pointed to the label under the photograph on the wall behind. 'That's who we're talking about – Councillor Leroy.'

And that's when I guessed what had happened. While we were leaning back against the wall to let the father with the pushchair pass, her head must have brushed against the photo. But if, from that, she knew he wouldn't be the one to give me the Harries Cup, she must have known what was going to happen to him. And I like Mr Leroy. He was so kind the year that Toby beat me, managing to make me smile even though I was close to crying. And Mrs Trent says he even remembered to ask after me when I wasn't there last year. I wouldn't like to think of him as ill. Or *worse*.

'So why won't he be there?'

Imogen said uneasily, 'Mel, I don't know. *Honestly.*'

I don't think I've ever heard anyone say the word 'honestly' more as if they were lying. But this was no time to start a quarrel. If I had raised my voice, it would have echoed up over the balcony, and Mum would have hurried down from the café to chew me out for being so rude to someone I'd invited.

Scowling, I turned away. And then I thought: Well, fair's fair. She might be hiding something, but there are things I don't tell her. She didn't know I liked her near me in the pool because the fact that she kept everyone away gave me more room to practise.

Cheered, I lifted my bag of swimming things. 'Come on,' I said, grabbing her arm. 'All this is wasting good swimming time. Let's hurry up and get changed, and get in the water so I can get on with my tumble turns.'

And, filled with relief at being let off the hook, she rushed after me through the swing doors.

CHAPTER TWELVE

Not that the great clear-a-space-around-us plan was working properly. It was so irritating. From the moment we stepped in the changing rooms, we were surrounded. First, Imogen got caught up in a game with the small children in the next cubicle.

'Knicker-snatcher! Knicker-snatcher!'

I heard them giggling the whole time I was getting into my swimsuit. And even as Imogen and I went through the tunnel to the footbaths, their squeals were echoing off the tiles.

But I was sure that, once we were in the water, everyone would drift away as usual. How wrong I was. Imogen splashed into the shallow end, gasping as she got used to the water, and suddenly she was being mobbed by excited children, all shrieking and calling to her, and it was obvious that if I was going to find room to practise, I'd do far better up the other end.

'See you in a bit.'

I looked up after every tumble turn, thinking her usual magic would have worked, and there'd be space around her. But it got worse. Each minute that passed, more children gathered, desperate to join in the game she was inventing. 'Can *I* play? Can *I* play?' And, by the time I'd finished practising, she even had a group of parents

94

floating lazily on their backs a few feet away from her, taking advantage of the fact that here in the pool today was the most brilliant unpaid nanny.

'Mel! Melly! Over here!'

She'd seen I'd finished. Still, I took my time, watching her curiously as I stroked my way through the water towards her. She looked like a different Imogen suddenly, standing taller, and swinging the children round, bursting with energy.

'Mel! Come and help! I *need* you.'

At her imperious command, I swam a little faster. But once I reached the circle, instead of joining it I arched up and plunged under to play the shark around the little forest of waving legs. Standing knee-deep in churning water shrieking with laughter is certainly not my idea of fun.

But no-one can stay for ever under water. So, in the end, I had to surface to face this merry, bright-eyed person who'd been turning things into a glorious play-time.

Just like her mother . . .

And that, of course, is when I realized. Splashing to her side, I pulled her round to face me. 'It's that *necklace*, isn't it?'

'Sorry?'

Peeling strands of wet hair from across her eyes, she stared.

'That necklace you're not wearing at the moment! That's what's making you—'

'Making me what?'

'You know.' There was no other way of putting it. '*Creepy*. You've taken it off, and now you're a different person. No-one would recognize you. Look at you! You're—'

But little hands were grabbing at her. She swung around to face a dozen shining wet faces, all yelling.

'Imogen, come back!'

'Swing me again!'

'Don't go off now!'

Imogen turned back to me, distracted and torn. 'That can't be right,' she said. 'Don't forget everything started *years* before I was given the necklace.'

'Yes, maybe it did,' I said. 'But—'

Then something made me stop – right there. Go carefully, I warned myself. If Imogen's mother can't see that she once had a totally different sort of daughter – ablaze with life – then she must really have her mind set on this magic stuff. Melly, you might have to sort all this out yourself. Don't forget Professor Blackstaffe says in his book that 'knowledge is power'. So maybe it's best not to give too much away.

'Oh, *right*!' I said. 'Stupid of me. I'd forgotten

you'd already had those visions earlier, when you were younger.'

She didn't notice anything suspicious. And anyway, the children were still clamouring. 'Imogen! Swing me!'

She picked up the nearest child and swung her round. Quickly, I copied her. 'Who wants the next go? Queue up! Queue up!'

As I said, standing in circles shrieking with merriment is not my idea of a good time. But I did stick it for a good half hour, rather than have Imogen even remember what it was that I'd just said before her little friends distracted her. Or begin to suspect what it was I was thinking.

CHAPTER THIRTEEN

Of course she thought that wearing the necklace had nothing to do with it. Imogen wasn't a reader. If you don't read, you don't get all that practice in picking up clues, and making up pictures in your head of how things must have happened. I'd suddenly imagined her exactly as she'd described herself when she was little, standing by the Christmas tree, sparkling all over because her cousin was hooking every glittery thing that he could find onto her somewhere.

Every glittery thing . . .

Then, just a couple of years later, in the very

same room, dancing a private princess dance for her mother. She'd have her tutu on, of course. And her pink ballet slippers. But to dress up to look the part, surely the first place she'd have gone was the old jewellery box. With the help of some hairgrips, even the slinkiest of gold chains can be made to look like a tiara.

And then, last year, on her birthday, what was she given? (Because around then is when she said all this started in earnest.) The very day she took the desk beside me, she'd said, 'My granny gave it to my mother, and now she's passed it on to me.'

I know my mother wouldn't pass on something like that, unless the day was very special.

What day's more special than your birthday?

'First, check your working,' Mr Hooper says. So, in the changing rooms, I asked her casually,

'What should I ask for on my birthday?'

'Melly, your birthday's not for *months*.'

'I know,' I said. 'But I like thinking about it. What did you get last year?'

Her eyes shone with the memory. 'A trip to London. We saw *Copacabana*!'

'Brilliant! What did you wear?'

'Well, we were in posh seats. So I wore my blue top and red velvet skirt.'

'What about jewellery?'

She thought back. 'Earrings. And my necklace,

of course, because I'd just been given that. Oh, yes. And my swirly snake ring.'

'*If there's time, check twice,*' says Mr Hooper. So on the way out of my cubicle, I pulled my new library book out of my bag and rested it on top, ready. Then I made sure that when Mum undid her handbag, I was at her side.

'Here you are, Mel,' she said, holding my watch out. But I ignored it totally, and slipped my hand inside her bag, to fish out the necklace.

Again, it was cold, and almost too slinky to the touch. I didn't drop it, though. I kept a grip as I held it out towards Imogen and pretended to stumble. And, as I fell, I laid my hand flat on the library book.

Wolf!

Such a howling! I could barely hear for baying in my ears. And sounds of yelping and snapping. It was *horrible*.

'Mel? Sweetheart?'

I'd sunk to my knees, my hand still flat on the book. Mum offered me the water bottle she was holding.

'You look quite faint, love. Have a sip of this.'

She pushed the water closer and I went berserk. Flailing out wildly, I dashed the plastic bottle from her hand and sent it rolling over the tiles.

'No!' I screamed. 'No! Get it away from me!'

'Mel, what's the *matter*?'

Mum's face was close, her arms were tight, and though they've told me since that I was screaming, inside my head it didn't sound like proper screams. More like a howling.

Mum kicked my bag away to drop beside me on the floor. 'Mel? Mel!'

At once, the shaking lessened. The awful noises in my ears began to fade. Imogen insisted after that it was only a few seconds at most before my echoing screams turned into sobs. I wouldn't know. The only way that I remember it, there were no sobs at all, just a horrible whining and whimpering, and, as I gradually realized that Mum was holding me and I was safe, the most peculiar leftover feeling of sick unease.

Mum pushed my hair from my face. 'Melly? Are you all right now? Can you walk?'

I shook off the last pricklings of terror.

'I'll be fine. Really.'

Imogen reached for my bag. 'I'll carry this.'

I nodded, and thrust the hateful necklace into her hand. 'Here, take this too.'

'Thanks.'

She rushed ahead to push at the revolving door. Mum kept her arm around me as I stumbled through. And I was glad that Imogen had already spilled out of the doorway into the car park, safely out of hearing, when Mum, still very worried, said to me, 'Mel, that was *terrifying*. You looked positively *haunted*.'

That night, still feeling shaky, I pulled *Wolf!* out of my bag and settled down to it. You don't have to be the greatest reader in the world to know what's coming. It was about a pack of wolves during the summer one of them caught hydrophobia

– a mortal fear of water. Even as I was reading, I could hear echoes of the ghastly howling deep in my head.

'*And, if it's really important,*' Mr Hooper says, '*and you have time, check it a third time.*' So maybe I really should have found some way to get the necklace in my hand again, and touch a photo, to see if, out of nowhere, I suddenly knew something I shouldn't.

But I couldn't face it. For one thing, it was obvious the necklace worked even more fiercely on strangers than on the people who owned it. When I touched *Wolf!*, it had whipped up a storm of a vision. If it had ever worked even one half as vividly for Mrs Tate or Imogen, they would have realized its powers in a flash.

Or . . .

It was the creepiest thought yet. Maybe the necklace recognized its enemies. Maybe it sensed when someone hated it and thought the whole idea of seeing the future was sick and horrible, and quite, quite wrong.

And I *do* think that. I truly do. Suppose I had a necklace like Imogen's, and touched a photo of someone in my family – Dad, say – and suddenly knew that something dreadful was going to happen to him before he came home on his next leave. I couldn't *bear* it. I'd go *mad*.

No, seeing the future is terrible. Crippling. It shouldn't be wished on anyone. And it was hardly Imogen's fault that her dad wasn't around any more, and her mother was the sort who preferred seeing things as 'interesting' or 'fun', to looking at them clearly.

It could be one of Professor Blackstaffe's little problems.

Someone you know has special
powers that make her life
horribly difficult.
  Do you:
    A: Put a stop to it any way you
       can?
    B: Not interfere, because it's a 'gift'
       she's been given?
    C: Hope things will work out
       right?

My mother would have been a definite *A*. She
had as good as said so.

I wasn't sure if Mrs Tate was *B* or *C*. I did
know one thing, though. They were both useless.
So I knew something else, too: it was up to me.

Chapter Fourteen

I had my doubts, though. Lots of people have a gift that makes life hard for them. Dennis has to do two hours on the piano every evening. Clive couldn't come on the French trip because his football coach said it was far too near the county trial. And Moira's parents have to drag her out of bed at five every morning to drive to the ice rink for her solo practice.

At least, though, most of the time, those three enjoy what they're doing. Poor Imogen might be happy enough lost in her daydreams on the little yellow tub in the book corner, but, when I thought about it, the only time I'd ever seen her truly happy was that time in the pool. Who would have thought that taking off a tiny gold chain could cause such a miracle of transformation? Like Snow White in her coffin when the bite of poisoned apple fell from her lips, Imogen had woken to her own real self – lively and noisy, and surrounded by friends (just exactly the sort of person Mr Hooper wishes I was!).

He is a teacher, so I asked him first.

'What is the word for one of those things that makes someone different?'

He looked at me as if I'd spoken to him in Greek. 'What *sort* of thing?'

'Sorry. I can't tell you that.'

'Well, what sort of "different"?'

I glanced at Imogen. 'Sorry. I can't tell you that, either.'

I knew exactly what was coming next.

'All right, Mel. Give me an *example*.'

I didn't want to say a word about gold, or even jewellery. But thinking about the necklace did remind me of the peculiar scratches on the gold. Water and roots, she'd said. So, just for an example, I picked one of those.

'Suppose it was some sort of root.'

'Some sort of *root*?'

It did sound a bit daft. 'All right,' I said hastily. 'Some kind of acorn. A silver acorn that's been lost for years. And, when it's found, everyone who touches it—'

Again, I hesitated. The last thing I wanted was to invite suspicion.

'Everyone who touches it can cook sausages perfectly!'

I'd certainly invited suspicion now.

'Melly,' Mr Hooper asked me, 'do you really think you ought to be in school today? Were you at all feverish this morning?'

I brushed his anxieties aside. 'What is it *called*?' I said. 'I *know* there has to be a word for it. What's it called? A magic something that makes people able to do things they can't do normally.'

'Oh, that!' he said. 'It's called a talisman. Or an amulet. They're both charmed objects. Both have magic powers.'

So it was back to the town library. And now, with the right words, I found my way through all the indexes, and through the lists on screens. And there was loads. A paragraph in this book, a whole chapter in that. Even a few sinister stories. In fact, from reading some, I started to see why these peculiar charmed objects were always being found in places like the darkest caverns and the deepest wells. They'd almost certainly been chucked there by the poor soul who'd had the rotten, miserable luck of being blessed with them before.

Because, all through my reading, one thing was absolutely clear as paint. My first, and worst, suspicion was the right one. For all she might love those magic moments in the book corner, dreaming of playing with puppies, or cantering through moonlight on snow-white steeds, Imogen would never be properly happy until she was rid of the necklace.

I sat in the library window-seat, chewing my nails, working out what to say to her. First, I'd explain about the necklace. Then I'd remind her of all the bad things about the gift, and how it was ruining her school life. And then I'd get her to agree that the best thing to do was—

'Up here? On this shelf? Oh, thank you!'

Over the other side of the tall shelving stacks, someone was speaking to the librarian.

I knew that breathless, eager voice. I peeped round the bookshelves. Yes! It was Imogen's mother. Around her shoulders was a wrap like an old-fashioned counterpane of bright sewn squares, and in her blazing hair were rows and rows of pretty pink plastic slides.

If she'd been my mother, I'd have crawled out of the library with my head in a bag. Instead, I watched her carefully. She drew down book after book, flicking through, peering at indexes in the back and returning them to the bookshelves. And then she settled on a large red book as big as a brick. Pulling a pencil out of the little bag dangling from her wrist, she copied a few words down on a scrap of paper, skipped a few pages, then copied down a few words more.

Then, looking satisfied, she slid the book back on the shelf and left.

I didn't take my eyes off its cover for one single second. So there was no mistake. I pulled the right book out.

And my heart sank. The book in my hand was called *Make More of Magic!*

So it was obvious that, to rescue poor Imogen, I was definitely going to have to get rid of the necklace myself. But how? You can't just snatch a gold chain from around someone's neck and hope they'll not notice. All week, the problem gnawed at me. I tried to slide the idea into her head of taking it off.

'Doesn't it irritate your skin a bit, wearing it all day?' I asked her.

'No,' she said cheerily. 'Mum used to find it scratchy. That's why she hardly ever wore it. But it doesn't bother me in the slightest.'

No hope there, then. So I tried something else. 'Well, don't you worry about losing it when we have sports, or in dancing?'

But she just shook her head. And since the only time I'd ever seen her take it off was at the pool when Mum persuaded her, I was stuck.

And stayed stuck. I couldn't, after all, invite her swimming again, and snaffle it then. Mum would end up in jail. But I was sure there had to be some way of parting Imogen from her necklace.

Twice that week I thought, I'll give up. It's not my problem. And twice, Mr Hooper picked her to fetch the set of reading books, *The Hunted*, out of the cupboard. The first time, she managed to bring them back in a pile balanced on her own workbook and slide them off, untouched, onto his desk. But it did cause an avalanche. So, next day, when he told her to fetch the books again, he added, 'And, this time, Imogen, try carrying them *sensibly*.'

111

She left her workbook on her desk, and carried the readers in a normal pile. Her hands were shaking, and her eyes were wide with fright.

'Really,' he said, quite sharply. 'All I said to you was "Carry them sensibly". There's no need to look as if I'm going to catch you and put you in the broth pot!'

So that was the ending of yet another book given away – another reading time spoiled. And Imogen didn't look too happy, either, at the ticking off. So I kept thinking, turning crazy, far-fetched plans over and over in my mind as the end of term crept steadily closer.

Imogen kept asking, 'Melly, is something wrong?'

And I'd say, 'Nothing. No. I was just thinking.'

'What about?'

'Nothing.'

And Mr Hooper soon climbed on my back as well.

'Is something worrying you, Mel? Are you getting nervous about the Harries Cup?'

It seemed as good an excuse as any for being too distracted to work properly. So, not exactly lying, I told him in an anxious voice, 'Well, there are only two days, three hours and five minutes before the race . . .'

He put his hand on my shoulder. 'Brace up! You won't have any problems. It's my guess that—'

Imogen swivelled hastily in her seat. 'Mr Hooper! You mustn't *say* that! *Anything* might happen!'

'Yes,' Tasj said, overhearing. 'Melly might get cramp.'

'Or meet a shark under water,' Luke offered helpfully.

'Or get her toe stuck in the pool drain,' suggested Maria.

Mr Hooper let out one of his great who'd-be-a-teacher groans. 'What *is* it about the people in this classroom? Why can't a teacher even have a private word with one of his pupils without everyone in earshot muscling in with their feeble jokes and half-witted suggestions!'

He turned to Imogen, to correct her work. And just as well, because one of those feeble jokes and half-witted suggestions had given me the best idea I'd had – the *only* idea I'd had in a whole week of solid thinking – of how to rescue Imogen and get rid of the necklace without either me or Mum being arrested for robbery.

Chapter Fifteen

Next morning, I hauled my gym mat onto the pile, and said to Miss Rorty, 'Did you hear about the swimming gala at Green Lane Primary?'

She pulled my mat straighter. 'No. What about it?'

'Tons of things lost,' I told her. 'Watches. Bracelets. Everything.'

'What, *stolen*?'

'No, no,' I assured her. 'Just fallen off in the water.'

'I don't see—'

'To find someone's tiny silver crucifix, they even had to drain the pool.'

'Drain the pool? Really?'

I added the clincher as I turned my back. '*And the school had to pay for it.*'

Her forehead wrinkled. 'Melly, where did you hear—?'

No way of answering that one. And the people behind were pushing. So I fled.

They only pinned up the notice the day before the race.

SWIMMING GALA

No watches or jewellery are to be worn tomorrow in the water. All swimmers are advised to leave their valuables at home.

'I'm just going to tuck my watch into my sock,' I said to Imogen. 'I know it'll be safe.'

'Do you think so?'

'Oh, yes. We're not out of the changing rooms that long. Especially people like you, who are only in the class relay.'

That set her off again, fretting about her one part in the gala – swimming her width.

'Will they mind if I'm the slowest?'

'You won't be slowest,' I assured her. 'Tasj will be slowest. She only learned to swim two weeks ago. And Colin Hamblebury's pretty useless. He just thrashes his arms about and never gets anywhere. And Liz doesn't put herself out much. So you'll probably even be faster than her.'

Imogen was still looking worried. 'You really do believe you have it taped, this swimming gala, don't you, Mel?'

'You bet,' I said, not mentioning that, this year, it was going to be more important than ever to judge it right. I'd worked out that I'd only have eight or so seconds' leeway before Toby Harrison would come steaming up behind, with Surina behind him, and at least one of the Trent twins after her. One clumsy dive, and I'd lose most of my head start. So I had two more things to practise now, and only one session in the pool to get both of them perfect before the big race.

'Nervous?' asked Imogen, but I wouldn't say. For one thing, although she only had one measly width to swim, each time I caught her eye, it seemed to me that she was still staring at me anxiously, and I didn't want to make her worse. And for another, she was the last person in the world I could confide in this time, because my plan to win the Harries Cup now included wasting six seconds getting rid of her necklace.

Six seconds exactly. I'd timed it. My new 'touch-the-bottom' tumble turn took four seconds longer than usual. And then you had to add on another two before I was back up to speed. It was still a dead cert, if not the romp home I'd wanted. But there seemed no way out. No point in explaining to anyone about the necklace if no-one was going to be tough enough to throw it away for good. For that was the only thing. All the books said so.

I could try and explain to her mother. The problem was, I wasn't sure what Mrs Tate would do. My mother would have taken a ferry out to sea, to drop the pesky thing deeper. But Mrs Tate was different. You only had to peek in her enchanted back garden with its secret dells and perky elves, or join in eating iced fairy cakes in one of her story-book tea times, to know she didn't really live in the sensible grown-up world where people look after their children properly and protect them from things that might damage them. Look how excited she already was about Imogen's weird powers – 'Anything "special" happen?' If I explained that I'd worked out that they came through the gold chain, instead of wanting to hurl it over a cliff into the sea, she'd more than likely clap her hands together and tell us it was *exactly* like something in one of her favourite old books, *Ellen's Enchanted Necklace*. She'd look up 'amulets' in *Make More of Magic!*, and want Imogen to keep it to see what would happen.

If Imogen ended up looking grey and haunted enough under the strain, then Mrs Tate might finally come to her senses and lock the chain safely away for a while. But not for long, I'd bet. After a bit, the memory of how it had chewed up her daughter's life would begin to fade round the edges. She'd soon forget how rotten Imogen's schoolwork had been, and how people used to move away when she came near, and how she could scarcely bear to touch some books, and daydreamed her life away when she picked up others.

And, one rainy day, out it would come again. 'Just in case you're a bit better at it, now that you're older,' or, 'Just in case, this time, it only tells you about *nice* things.'

But I'm not tired and distracted. And I can open any book I like without jumping for fright, or acting as if the pages have scorched me. And, over the week, I had been reading up on all sorts of magic rings and lamps and mirrors and swords and boots and wands and crystals, and even pebbles. I'd found a dozen stories called things like *The Amulet in the Wood*, and *The Silver Talisman,* and *Sasha's Charmed Bracelet*, and *The Enchanted Cap of Gold.*

And I'd learned this. You weren't free till you threw whichever horrible thing it was away.

As far as possible. Firmly. For good, for sure, and for *ever*.

CHAPTER SIXTEEN

So I said nothing. Nothing to Mum, when she made me my favourite pancakes for breakfast – 'to stoke me up properly'. Nothing to Dad, who must have put his alarm on in the middle of the night to phone and wish me luck from Singapore. And nothing when people looked up as I walked in the classroom, and asked, 'Are you nervous, Mel?' or, 'Getting excited?'

'A bit,' was all I answered, as if the Harries Cup was the one thing on my mind, not jewellery theft, and spoiling a perfectly good friendship. And I kept my cool front up all through the morning, and all through lunch, and on the walk to the pool. When Miss Rorty winked at me during the Grand Opening, I winked back. I tried not to worry as I inspected Councillor Archibald Leroy for signs of a possible heart attack. And when we were sent off to change, straight after the fourth years, I made as many jokey faces as everyone else while Miss Rankin prowled round the cubicles, fussing and scolding.

'Hurry up. There are still loads of people to come through these changing rooms. Don't leave so much as a sock in the cubicles. Put your stuff neatly on the benches.'

Her eyes fell on Imogen's pile. 'And *sensibly*, please, Imogen.'

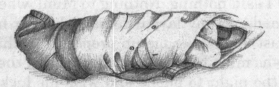

I could see why she'd said it. Imogen had rolled up her uniform into a giant sausage. Clearly, she'd taken my advice and hidden the necklace inside it. But even without looking, I would have known she wasn't wearing it, because the first thing Miss Rankin did as she scolded was drop both hands cheerfully onto her shoulders to push her back to her clothes pile. And only a moment later, Maria slid an arm in hers. 'Hey, Immy. Ready to break the world water speed record?'

Imogen turned to me. 'Coming?'

I nodded, and, as a trio, we splashed through the footbath into the brightness of the pool and huddled round one of the radiators, waiting for Mrs Parkin to get round to calling out our first big race.

It wasn't long.

'Inter-Class Relay! Mr Hooper's, Mrs Potter's and Ms Robinson's classes. Half of you on each side, please. One width each!'

Our class always puts the weedy swimmers on first, to get them over. Tasj started us off, and she was absolutely useless, as usual. Then Colin Hamblebury fell in and thrashed his arms about a bit, losing us half a width more. And Liz hadn't improved much. She just stroked her way across idly, not even bothering to glance to the side to see how the other two classes were doing.

But Imogen did brilliantly. She ended up swimming against Norman Pizarro and Tara Bloor, neither of whom are much good. But still she made up miles in her short width, and when she

got out of the water, everyone was cheering.
  'Well done, Immy!'
  'Excellent swim, Miss Mermaid!'

She looked delighted. And I was really pleased as well, because it showed that what I had in mind was right. It couldn't have been more than a few minutes since she'd taken off the necklace, and look! Already she seemed to have melted in and become just like one of the others. She was laughing and joking, and huddling round the radiator as if she were just one more companionable bee in a hive. They'll be plaiting her hair next, I remember thinking. And, just for a moment, I wondered if I would be jealous when it was all over, and she was in a gang with them, and no longer a loner like I am.

And, no, I thought. I really don't think that I'll give a hoot. It seems to me that you can only get truly jealous of people if they are somehow exactly the way you've always wanted to be (or think you are already, but others don't realize).

But I don't want to be what Mr Hooper calls, 'a little more gregarious'.

I just want to be me.

And Imogen should have the right to be her real self, too. So seeing her leaning back against the radiator, laughing, with the wet ends of her hair being flicked by Hal, made it easier to sneak away, back through the footbaths into the crowded changing rooms, where even Miss Rankin had lost track of who was coming and going.

'Excuse me . . . Can I get through please? . . . Sorry . . .' Finally I made it past the busy cubicles back to the bench. I glanced round quickly, then slid my fingers inside Imogen's tightly wrapped pile of clothes. And all I can say is that I hope she makes a better job of hiding the next piece of jewellery somebody gives her.

The glittering loops of this one practically fell into my hand.

And it was the weirdest thing. Suddenly I felt

as if I were already underwater – way, way down, lost in a storm of bubbles.

'Oh!'

I clawed at my throat. I couldn't breathe and my knees were buckling beneath me.

'Are you all right?' A little second year had heard me gasping. 'Shall I go and get Miss Rankin for you?'

I was so close to fainting that I dropped the necklace, which fell in a fold of towel. Only then did I manage to gather my senses.

'No, no. I'm fine,' I said, even before the wave of panic passed, leaving me even more sure I had to get this horrid chain of Imogen's out of our lives. Not even caring whose towel it was I was borrowing, I scrunched the necklace up in it as tightly as I could without touching, and pushed my way through all the second years rushing out of the cubicles, to hurry back the way I'd come, towards the footbaths.

And how I thought I might intimidate a golden chain with my determination, I'll never know. (I'm not in the habit of talking to jewellery.) But as I splashed through the arch, I found myself whispering to it, horribly fiercely:

'Don't think you're going to beat *me*. Because you're *not*!'

I heard a voice behind me. 'Keep your hair on, Mel. Only a race.'

I spun round. Stepping out of the footbaths on the boys' side was Toby Harrison, who'd win the Harries Cup for sure if I weren't swimming.

'I didn't mean you,' I said hastily.

He looked offended. 'I'm sure I don't know who you *do* mean, then.'

How can you try and explain you're talking to a necklace? You can't. So I shut up, except to say, 'Well, good luck, anyway.'

He grinned. 'And good luck to you, Melly. See you at the finish – when I look back over my shoulder!'

'Keep dreaming, Toby!'

He went off towards his friends, and I stuffed the towel under the heating pipe, and hurried back to join our relay queue. It had become so short that people were panicking.

'Mel, where have you *been*?'

'We thought you'd *vanished*.'

'We still have nearly half a width to make up. You can do it, can't you?'

Can I save half a width? Can Granny knit? I did the fastest racing dive Miss Rorty says she's ever seen in a school gala. I was across the pool so fast that poor Hugh Gregory had no idea his class had lost till he shook the hair from his eyes and saw my fingertips already on the ledge, and me turning, laughing.

'But I was—'

127

I didn't hear the end for cheers.
'Brilliant, Mel!'
'*Saved!*'
I did a celebratory backwards flip in the water.
I thought I might as well. I knew I wasn't going
to beat any speed records winning the Cup race –

not with the tumble turn that I'd been practising up at the deep end. As soon as Miss Rorty saw that, she'd stop all her cheery nodding and waving. She'd be too busy wondering what on earth could have happened to turn a race that should have been a dead cert from the very start into a risky business with only three seconds to spare.

But there was no way round it. And I would at least still win the Cup. In my last practice session I'd timed it over and over. Four extra seconds for the tumble turn, and two more to get up to speed.

It could be done. And I'd do it.

And the best thing was that I couldn't possibly be tempted to fiddle with the plan. How could I? It was all worked out. Only one way to do it. Start from the shallower end, and, in a three-length race, you only get one tumble turn under the boards.

Or – put it another way – only one chance.

CHAPTER SEVENTEEN

Miss Rorty held the whistle between her teeth and looked down the line. Eight of us on our starting blocks. And me already shivering because, to get the right one, I'd had to take my place ages before.

'Ready?'

She raised an eyebrow because I wasn't in my usual stance. But finally, after about a billion years, she blew the whistle.

I lost the first two seconds then and there.

You try it. Try a racing dive, flinging yourself out over the water, stretching so thin you cut air. Then try it with one hand clamped to your hip to stop a slinky, cunning gold chain wriggling out of your swimsuit and landing on the tiles to shriek '*Stolen!*' at everyone and shame you for ever.

You'd have played safe like I did, and done a bellyflop too.

But in the huge, embarrassing splash of it, I did at least manage to hook out the chain. I couldn't do my usual strong spading through the water with it grasped in my hand. So it took time even to pull ahead of four particular pairs of feet I've never seen in front of me in my life, and reach the deep end. By then, at least, I'd even managed to pass the slower of the twins. But Toby and Surina were well ahead. And even Josh Murphy was thundering along at a good pace.

But I still had to do my stupid tumble turn. It might sound mad, but what was mostly in my mind was the thought of poor Miss Rorty who'd spent so much time training and encouraging me, and knew how important this race had become, and how much I wanted to win it. I knew she'd be standing at the edge, filled with dismay, wondering what on earth had happened to her best swimmer. First, that dreadfully clumsy starting dive; then the ham-fisted way I was ploughing through the water with one hand firmly clenched. And, now, coming up, the worst tumble turn she could imagine.

But there was no way round it. Instead of tucking up my legs and twisting fast to kick off straight and hard the way I'd come, I was about to waste even more time swimming down to the bottom.

To drop the necklace down the drain, where it would lie till, in the next water change, it would be swept into the sewers and out to sea.

Out of our lives for ever. Just like in the books.

And now the pool end was within my reach. Gathering myself into a ball, I tumbled perfectly, as I've been taught, and practised for so many hours. And, though it sounds crazy, even as I was doing it, I felt the necklace stir in my hand as if . . .

I have to say it. As if it *knew*.

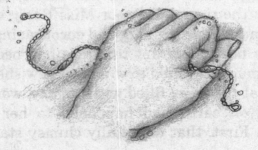

And then the battle started. All round me there blew up that storm of bubbles I'd sensed before. At first, I thought they must be mine. I thought I must be letting out my breath – too fast, too soon.

But it was nothing to do with me. It was the necklace. Even in all that cool water, the thing was scalding my fingers. Twisting and burning, trying to distract me, trying to make me let it go – *anything* rather than let itself be fed through one of the tiny squares of the drain grille and dropped out of sight for ever. That spiteful little chain of gold put up the worst fight. The water churned so fiercely I could barely see. My right hand burned so badly that, if I'd had breath to spare, I would have yelped.

But I was suddenly furious. It was so *unfair*. I'd trained for months to win the Harries Cup. I didn't ask Imogen Tate to come to our school. I didn't ask Mr Hooper to put her next to me – in fact I as good as begged him *not* to!

And just because I'd tried to fit in with what everyone wanted – be friendly, not hide in my books, get interested in real life for a change – everything had gone sour. And even swimming, the only other thing I liked and was good at, was being spoiled.

You can't talk under water. You lose your air in

133

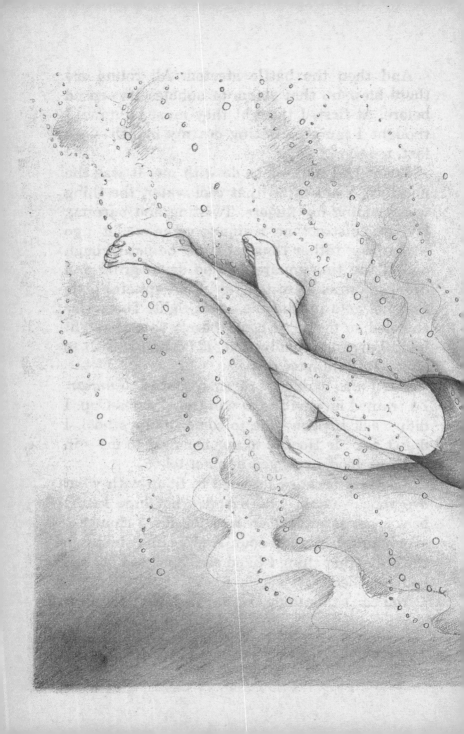

one large, glistening flood of bubbles. But if I could, I would have said it over again to Imogen's horrible necklace.

'Don't think you're going to beat *me*. Because you *won't*!'

Instead, I put my energy into one last enormous pull through the water. Clutching the chain, I swam down through the blizzard of angry bubbles till there, at last, I saw the drain.

And slammed my hand down flat. I didn't trust the necklace not to wriggle off. I rubbed the links of it over the grille till suddenly I felt the coils vanishing beneath my fingers as it went down. Now, under the flat of my palm, I could feel nothing but the clasp, a hard metallic lump still stubbornly clinging to the grille edge. And that's when I had to make the worst decision of my life.

'Come on!' I tried to tell myself. 'That's it. You've done it. Swim back up, quick. There's still a chance. You could still do it. You could still win the Harries Cup.'

But that old clasp was hanging on. And I knew why. Oh, I'd swim off, thinking I'd done the job and Imogen was safe. But the necklace would beat me. The clasp would cling on to the grille till evening session – Intermediate Diving. One after another for an hour, Miss Pollard's pupils would be plunging down. Someone was bound to spot it. I could hear them now.

'Miss Pollard! Miss Pollard! Look what I've found trapped in the drain. It must belong to someone in the gala.'

She'd reach down to take it. 'It looks quite valuable. I'd better drop it by the school tomorrow.'

No need to guess the rest. By break time, it would be back round Imogen's neck, strangling her life.

Professor Blackstaffe would have put it plainly enough.

To do something seriously important for a friend, you have to make a sacrifice.
   Do you:
   A: Do it?
   B: Kid yourself your thing matters just as much?

A cup's a cup. It might be made to matter in a book. But it's not serious. Not like real life.

So I just did it – used up my very last spare second or two prising that hateful, stubborn little clasp off the drain grille, and pushing it through. I'd run out of air. My lungs were on fire. But I still stayed to watch it sink – down, down, resentfully, till it was out of sight.

And then, at last, I let myself push away, up like an arrow. Breaking the surface, I took the very deepest breath, and stormed off after the others. I don't think I've ever in my life swum any faster. I pounded along, meeting the others coming back the other way for their third and last length.

I turned just as Surina reached the half-way mark. It was a brilliant tumble – fast and strong.

I knew at least Miss Rorty would be pleased to see I hadn't let her training down in front of everyone. It was my best turn ever.

I slid through the water like a needle through silk. First I saw Surina's toes, and then her knees, and then, since she was tiring, with one last great heave, I spun ahead. I took my next breath on the other side, to check the enemy. And, to my surprise, saw I'd left the other twin behind as well, and one more pull would bring me up to Toby.

I'm a machine in water when I'm pounding hard. Miss Rorty says it's like watching pistons in the engine of a great ship, or valves in a power station. I pulled on and on. And if the Harries Cup had only been a race one metre longer, there is not a shred of doubt I would have won it.

As it was, I lost.

CHAPTER EIGHTEEN

They were all there for me, I'll give them that. Miss Rorty wrapped a towel round me so fast that only she and I knew when she pressed the corner of it to my face, she wasn't blotting my hair at all, only stemming my tears of rage and frustration.

Toby didn't crow. All he said was, 'Jeez, that was close! Just two more seconds, Mel, and you'd have done it.'

Mr Hooper came up and hugged me even before he shook Toby's hand. Then he grinned ruefully. 'Oh, blimey. Now we're going to have to exhume poor Mrs Harries so she can change the age rules on her Cup race.'

And Maria said she saw Councillor Leroy whispering to his wife before she slipped out for a moment. And that it wasn't just a mistake that the brand new award – Best Overall Swimmer – had been left off the programme. She says the pool keeps fat round medals like the one he gave to me behind the counter as spares in case of dead heats in competitions.

So I knew what they all thought. And it was comforting. But not the same, even if everyone was cheering and stamping and giving me the thumbs up all the way back to the changing rooms. Because it was the Cup I wanted. And Mr Hooper can joke about digging up Mrs Harries all he likes, but it's over now. Finished. No prize is the same if the people who organize it have to change the rules so you can win it. Who wants that?

But it was worth it, I suppose – not that you'd think it from the way Imogen turned on me in the changing rooms.

First, she was just a bit panicked.

'My necklace! Where's it *gone*?'

'Isn't it there?'

'No!' She rooted through her clothes pile in a frenzy, tossing and shaking everything. 'It's *vanished*.'

She looked up wildly. All around us, people were gathering up their piles of clothes and making for the cubicles.

'Please!' she called. 'Everyone look for my necklace. It's disappeared.'

Maria was in there like a flash, of course. 'Miss Rorty said we weren't to—'

'I know what Miss Rorty said!' Imogen snapped. 'I *know*. I have *ears*. But *Melly* said—'

She broke off and turned to look at me. You could see the first glimmer of suspicion. 'Mel said she was quite sure it would be safe . . .'

I had to try and pretend I cared. 'What's *that* supposed to mean?'

'You know.'

'No,' I said. 'I'm afraid I don't.' I turned my back on her. I think I was really rather hoping she'd back off and leave me alone after my disappointment. But I was wrong.

'You *must* know, Melly.'

I tried to sound outraged. 'Me? Why *me*?'

'Be*cause*,' she hissed, 'you were the only one who knew my necklace was wrapped up in there.' Her eyes narrowed. 'In fact,' she added, 'now I come to think, you were the one who suggested I left it there in the first place.'

That's when I panicked a little. 'What would I want with your stupid necklace?'

Her eyes flashed. Her voice rose. 'You tell me, Mel! All I know is, you've taken an interest in it from the start. Practically the first thing you ever said to me was how much you liked it. *And* you asked if it was precious, and said you didn't think you'd ever be given anything that valuable yourself.'

Mirrors run all the way along the wall above the benches. Even the people with their backs to us could see I was blushing. The whole, huge, echoing changing room had fallen quiet.

Except for us.

'You really think I took it?'

She stared deep in my eyes. 'Yes,' she said. 'Yes, I do. In fact, I'm sure you did. I think you've hidden it somewhere and you'll sneak back for it later. And I think that's why you lost your stupid, *stupid* race, Mel. Because you were too busy planning to steal my necklace — or too guilty after doing it — to swim your fastest.'

And wasn't I tempted, then, to spoil everything I'd done to save her from her horrible necklace! 'I haven't got it!' I could have said to her. 'But I will tell you that while I was swimming in my stupid,

stupid race, I did see something glittery lying at the bottom of the pool, right by the drain.'

That would have fixed her. They'd have found it and given it back to her in no time.

And I was tempted. Very, very tempted. But I just gritted my teeth and thought of what Professor Blackstaffe would have said if he had overheard me. And at least I was sure now that I hadn't thrown away the Cup for nothing. She'd *never* find the necklace. She just doesn't read enough. If she read books, she'd understand that people live their *own* lives – lives completely special to them. They have their own things that matter, their own ways of going about them, and their own words to talk about them if they want. They don't go through their lives like plastic counters moving round a board game, each one a bit different on the surface so you can tell them apart, but all the same inside. I wanted to shake her. 'Look at me!' I wanted to shout. 'Look at me! Hello! It's *Mel* here, speaking. *Mel!* You know! This person you've sat next to for five whole weeks, and call a friend. This person who's spent *three whole years* wanting to win a race. Do you really think I'd toss the whole lot over just to take the chance to snatch a stupid necklace I wouldn't even be able to wear? *Do* you? *Do* you?'

But what was the point in setting Imogen off

thinking? Pushed, she might just work out why someone like me might *really* want to take her necklace.

Then she'd be one step nearer to working out where it was.

No. At least till the pool had been drained, it was best to say nothing.

CHAPTER NINETEEN

But everyone else talked. Toby Harrison set it all off by accident, mentioning we'd wished one another good luck coming out of the footbaths.

'So maybe Imogen's right,' someone as gossipy as Maria must have said. 'After all, what was she doing back there again ten minutes later?'

And tongues began to wag. People remembered that I'd disappeared till almost the end of the relay. And then the little girl whose towel I'd borrowed without asking popped up to mention she'd found it hidden under the hot water pipes. Had Imogen looked for her necklace there?

And that's when Mr Hooper got involved.

'So, Mel,' he said, coming up behind me after next morning's Assembly. 'Time for a little chat?'

'I suppose so.'

He didn't take me to the classroom. Instead, he dropped a hand on my shoulder and steered me down to the quiet end of the corridor. Then he leaned back against the door.

'About this necklace that Imogen shouldn't even have been wearing in the first place . . .' was how he began.

At least that made it easier for me to lift my head.

'I know how it looks,' I said. 'And I know what she's been saying. But, honestly, I never wanted it and I haven't got it.'

No lies in that, so it came out sounding the truth, and he believed it.

'So what were you doing back in the changing rooms?'

'I was so nervous that I . . . I needed to . . .' Again, I stopped, and he assumed I was too embarrassed to finish the sentence.

'And what about little Fay Tucker's towel?'

'That was me,' I confessed. 'I was frozen. I was shivering all over. I saw it lying there, and I know it was wrong, but, with the big race coming up, I thought . . .'

'You thought it was important and, if she knew, she wouldn't mind?'

He hadn't said *what* I thought was important. So what he'd said was true, in its own way.

'That sort of thing.'

He eyed me steadily. 'Well, Mel,' he said. 'I've known you ever since you were in first year and, as far as I know, you've never snitched so much as a Snoopy rubber from anyone – except from under their nose to start a fight. So I'm going to choose to believe you.'

'I expect you'll be the only one,' I couldn't help saying.

He shrugged. 'I'm not so sure about that.' And then he grinned. 'Now if it had been a *book* she'd accused you of pinching . . . But a *necklace*. Oh, I'm not so sure about that.'

And I did suddenly feel a little hope. That's true, I thought. I've been here years and years, and they all know me. But Imogen has only been here for a matter of weeks, and they're so used to thinking she's a little strange, it might turn out quite easy for them to just assume she's wrong as well.

And that's exactly how it all worked out. Maria told me, after. 'As soon as Mr Hooper had made that excuse to send you off to the staffroom with those keys, he started on at us about how very unlikely it was that someone who'd never even bothered to wear rings or bracelets or anything, would care two hoots about a silly necklace.'

'Did he say "silly"? Did he really?'

'Well, no. But you could sort of hear it in his voice. And Imogen was furious, you could tell, as if, just because she and her mother think you stole her precious necklace, we all have to think that too. She sat there with a stony look. And, after, she said that she was going to ask her mum if she could go back to her old school.'

149

'Really?'

'That's right. She says that after the gala she bumped into several of her old classmates, and they were really nice to her. And *they* believe her.'

'So she's going back next term?'

'No. Sooner than that. Next week, she hopes. She doesn't even want to come back to us tomorrow.'

'Leaving so soon!'

It just popped out, because there was one last thing I had to do. Edging past Maria, I pelted off to the book corner. On the top shelf, crammed in between *The Bumper Book of Ghost Stories* and *Weird Tales II*, was *Lucy Fainlight.*

It looks like nothing as a book. The picture on the cover is just a girl in a crinoline skirt. She looks quite drippy, as if nothing of any interest could ever happen to her. The book's so old, it has that tiny print everyone hates reading because it takes for ever to get down a page. The paragraphs go on for *days*, and there are only three pictures, and they're all hidden behind tissue. Probably the only reason it's still on the shelf is because it was donated by Mrs Trent's own granny.

But it's the creepiest book I've ever read. It's terrifying. Horrible. From the first page, your skin starts crawling. I'm not even going to begin to tell you what happens to poor Lucy Fainlight. But it's a ghastly story.

"Again she heard it!"

Outside the classroom, I bumped into Toby.

'Do me a favour,' I begged him. 'Give this book to Imogen.'

He gave me a funny look. 'The buzzer's gone. Aren't you coming in?'

'Not right this minute.'

Shrugging, he took the book. On his way over to his place by the window, he dropped it in front of Imogen.

'Here,' he said. 'Present from Melly.'

I thought that might be a mistake. She might ignore it. But, no. Clearly curious, she glanced at it, then, gingerly as usual, reached out to turn it over so she could see the picture on the front. I stood in the doorway, watching and waiting as her fingers touched the cover.

And nothing happened. Not a thing. No draining face. No trembling fingertips. No growing look of dismay. She might as well have been inspecting a cauliflower for all the emotion she displayed.

That's when I knew I'd done it. The girl who only had to lean back against a photo on a wall to know exactly who was going to win the Harries Cup now didn't even have the first inklings of a clue what horrors lay in store for Lucy Fainlight. Now she was free. Free from pretending she didn't know things that she did. Free from half-lies and horrible decisions (like having to let me worry about nice Mr Leroy because she couldn't bring herself to tell me that it wasn't that he wouldn't be on the podium to hand me the Cup. It was that I wouldn't be there to take it!).

And free to have surprises. Read books without knowing the end. Go back to her old school and be delighted at just how quickly and easily she could make friends. She would be happy, the miseries of the future no longer dripping like poisonous rain into the days of here and now, spoiling her life.

She would be free.

And so would I. I could barely believe it. Free to sneak off and read, just like before. Free to hide back in books. Free from the shackles of having to sit by someone at lunch, and on trips, and before Assembly.

153

Free to unplug from the chatter and blot them all out, as usual. Free to be *me*.

It only took Mr Hooper half a day to suss me out.

'Melly, you have the most seraphic smile on your face. Go on. Admit it. You're delighted to have this desk beside you back empty.'

He raised the lid, and saw that I'd colonized it already with half the new stock from the library.

He raised his eyebrows at me.

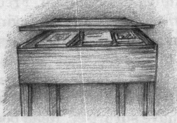

'It's only sensible,' I told him. 'It's only if you've read them that you know exactly which section you should put them in.'

'Oh, I see,' he said. 'It's not just that you're planning a long and pleasant convalescence from the strain of having a friend for a few days.'

I showed my outrage. 'She was here *six whole weeks*.'

He shook his head. 'Oh, Melly, Melly. I've said it before. What on earth are we going to do with you?'

'Nothing,' I told him firmly. 'Just don't fret. I've *told* you. I've told *everyone*. I'm happy reading. I prefer the company of books.'

'You really won't miss her, will you?'

'No,' I said. 'I really won't.'

And it is true. I'm not sorry that she's gone. I wish her well. I hope her mum gets over the disappointment. I have felt a tiny bit uneasy once or twice, mostly because it was meddling. But if I had to face the same choice over again, I'd still pick *A*, even if Professor Blackstaffe were standing there scowling. I'd still do exactly what I did.

So, truthfully, I only have one real regret. And that's that the very first time I came across something in real life halfway as exciting as something in a story, I was the one who put a stop to it. I was the one who, when you think about it, closed it up.

I'd never have done that with a book. But there again, as I explained right at the start, that's just the way I am. I have *always* preferred reading.

Anne Fine was born in Leicester. She went to Wallisdean County Primary School in Fareham, Hampshire, and then to Northampton High School for Girls. She read Politics and History at the University of Warwick and then worked as an Information Officer for Oxfam before teaching (very briefly!) in a Scottish prison. She started her first book during a blizzard that stopped her getting to Edinburgh City Library and has been writing ever since.

Anne Fine is now a hugely popular and celebrated author. Among the many awards she has won are the Carnegie Medal (twice), the Whitbread Children's Novel Award (twice), the Guardian Children's Literature Award, a Smarties Prize, and she has twice been voted Children's Writer of the Year.

She has written over forty books for children and adults, including *Goggle-Eyes*, *Flour Babies*, *Bill's New Frock*, *The Tulip Touch* and *Madame Doubtfire* (which was made into a feature film by Twentieth Century Fox, starring Robin Williams). In 1999, she was one of three people shortlisted for the new post of Children's Laureate.

Bad Dreams is Anne's second book to be published by Corgi Yearling Books; her first, *Charm School*, was shortlisted for the Sheffield Children's Book Award.

Anne Fine lives in County Durham and has two daughters and a large hairy dog called Henry.

The More the Merrier

ANNE FINE

Christmas comes but once a year. Luckily . . .

The Christmas holiday is, traditionally, a time
when families gather together. In Ralph s case,
this means ten or more relatives coming
to stay, including assorted aunts and uncles,
nutty Great-Aunt Ida and his ghastly cousins:
Titania in her sick-making, frilly, fairy dresses,
and twins Sylvester and Sylvia (it took till
Easter last year before the family dog
got over them).

Jammed into one small house for three days
of merriment and family fun, Uncle Tristram
hurling potatoes at the cat and Mum on the
verge of a breakdown, it soon becomes
obvious that, in this house, more definitely
does not mean merrier . . .

CORGI YEARLING
0 440 86585 9

Anne Fine

Illustrated by Ros Asquith

CORGI YEARLING BOOKS

CHARM SCHOOL AND BAD DREAMS
A CORGI YEARLING BOOK 0 552 55405 7

This edition first published in Great Britain for Scholastic by Corgi Yearling,
an imprint of Random House Children s Books, 2005

1 3 5 7 9 10 8 6 4 2

CHARM SCHOOL
First published in Great Britain by Doubleday, 1999
Copyright ' Anne Fine, 1999
Illustrations copyright ' Ros Asquith, 1999

BAD DREAMS
First published in Great Britain by Doubleday, 2000
Copyright ' Anne Fine, 2000
Illustrations copyright ' Susan Winter, 2000

The right of Anne Fine to be identified as the author of this work has been
asserted in accordance with the Copyright, Designs and Patents Act 1988.

Papers used by Random House Children s Books are natural, recyclable products
made from wood grown in sustainable forests. The manufacturing processes
conform to the environmental regulations of the country of origin.

Corgi Yearling Books are published by Random House Children s Books,
61—63 Uxbridge Road, London W5 5SA,
a division of The Random House Group Ltd,
in Australia by Random House Australia (Pty) Ltd,
20 Alfred Street, Milsons Point, Sydney, NSW 2061, Australia,
in New Zealand by Random House New Zealand Ltd,
18 Poland Road, Glenfield, Auckland 10, New Zealand,
and in South Africa by Random House (Pty) Ltd,
Endulini, 5A Jubilee Road, Parktown 2193, South Africa

THE RANDOM HOUSE GROUP Limited Reg. No. 954009
www.kidsatrandomhouse.co.uk

A CIP catalogue record for this book is available from the British Library.

Printed and bound in Great Britain by
Cox & Wyman Ltd, Reading, Berkshire

CHAPTER ONE

'I can't choose anything,' wailed Bonny, tossing the brochure on the floor. 'Not out of this horrible lot. Why can't I just stay here?'

'Oh, yes,' scoffed her mother. 'Spend the whole day alone here, in a house where the furniture hasn't even arrived yet. Next door to people we haven't even met, who might be axe-murderers. Oh, yes!' She picked up the brochure. 'Now, quickly, sweetheart. Choose one of the classes, or I'll have to choose one for you.'

Bonny snatched the brochure and went down the list again. 'Copperplate Handwriting!' she groaned. 'Practical Parenting! Defensive Driving! And Charm School!' She hurled it back down. 'All right, all right! I've chosen. I'll do Practical Parenting.'

'You can't do that. It says you need a baby.'

'I'll borrow one.'

'Don't be silly. You haven't even met anyone your own age yet. How could you find a *baby*?' Her mother glanced impatiently at her watch. 'Now listen, Bonny. We haven't time for any more of this. We have to leave now. This new job's important to me. I only have one day to brush up my accounting skills and pass the test to get my certificate. And my class starts at nine. So choose now. *Choose.*'

Bonny scowled horribly. The packing. The move. Losing her friends. A whole empty summer yawning in front of her, with absolutely no company, before starting again in a strange school. She was as miserable as she could be.

'Why can't I just come with you?'

'What? To Bookkeeping (Advanced)? You don't know anything at all about bookkeeping.'

It sounded so babyish to say, 'The way I feel, I'd rather just sit next to you all day, not understanding anything, than be sent off to do something of my own.' Instead, Bonny said sullenly:

'So? I don't even know what copperplate handwriting is, I'm too young to drive, and I may never have a baby.'

Her mother laughed and reached for the car keys. 'You know what this means, don't you, Bonbons?'

'No,' said Bonny. 'No, no, no.' She kicked out at the bright pink sheet of paper that had fallen from the brochure.

'No!' she said again. 'I am not going to Charm School.'

'Get in the car.'

'No,' said Bonny. 'Not if you paid me forty million pounds. Not if you boiled me in oil. Not if you begged me with tears rolling down your cheeks like pearls.'

'Get in the car.'

'If you do this to me,' Bonny warned her mother, 'I'll never speak to you again. I won't take out the rubbish. I won't make you pots of tea when you're tired. I won't bring home any of the notes from school. And I'll grow up to be a round-the-world yachtswoman, so you won't just have to worry about me for a few hours now and then. You'll have to worry about me *day* and *night*.'

'Charming!' said Mrs Bramble.

'See?' Bonny said desperately. 'I am already charming. I don't *need* lessons in it.'

Mrs Bramble glanced at her watch for the last time. 'This discussion is over,' she warned. 'I have a job to keep, so get in the car and sit on it quietly before I smack it!'

The woman behind the desk peered doubt-fully at Bonny's scowl and Bonny's faded jeans.

'Charm School? Are you sure? To me, she looks a little more like Woodwork I, or Starting French.'

'French only lasts an hour,' said Mrs Bramble. 'And Woodwork I doesn't begin till tomorrow. It's all today we need.'

Seeing the puzzled look on the woman's

face, she went on to explain.

'You see, I'm just starting a new job and I need to learn better accounting skills. And her father's still sitting in a lay-by with a broken down furniture van. And obviously she hasn't had any time to make any new friends yet—'

'I don't want new friends,' Bonny interrupted sourly. 'I want my old friends back.'

Mrs Bramble bit her lip, then bravely carried on. 'And what with the telephone not working yet, it wasn't possible to find a sitter. So ...'

She peered anxiously at her daughter, who glared back in a mixture of irritation and humiliation.

'Still ...' the woman said, still doubtful. '*Charm* School ...?'

'That's all there is,' said Mrs Bramble. 'Apart from Copperplate Handwriting. Unless you let her off the baby ...'

'Oh, no,' the woman said. 'You can't do Practical Parenting without a baby. You have to bathe it, you see.' She gave Bonny a nervous glance, as if she feared someone who looked as sullen and resentful as Mrs Bramble's daughter would just as soon drown a baby as wash it nicely behind the ears. 'One all-day Charm School it is, then,' she said, taking the money. 'And one all-day Bookkeeping (Advanced).'

She handed over the tickets. 'You'd better hurry,' she warned Mrs Bramble. 'Bookkeeping always starts dead on time. Don't worry about your daughter. I'll point her in the right direction.'

Mrs Bramble pecked Bonny hastily on the cheek. 'Bye, sweetheart. See you later.'

And she fled.

The woman ushered Bonny into the lift. 'You might as well take it,' she said. 'Even though you're not carrying any of the usual stuff.'

'The usual stuff?'

But just at that moment the lift doors closed, and Bonny found she was talking to herself.

Bonny got out of the lift on the third floor, as she'd been told, and stamped her foot.

'Horrible!' she muttered. 'Horrible, horrible, horrible! I hate this town. I hate this place. I hate the world. I hate everybody!'

'Wrong floor, I think,' a voice beside her said.

Bonny spun round and told the man hurrying round the corner into the lift, 'This is three, isn't it? Where I'm supposed to be?'

He looked her up and down. 'I don't think so, Little Miss Grumpy. Unless, of course, you're here to help Maura with the sound and the lighting. The only other people on this floor today are Mrs Opalene's pupils.'

'That's right,' Bonny said stubbornly. 'And I'm one of them.'

'Oh, yes?' As if to show how little he believed her, he put his foot in the lift doorway to stop it closing. 'So where's all your stuff?'

A tinned voice spurted out of the lift ceiling. *'Please check the doors for obstructions.'*

Startled, the man drew back his foot. The lift doors closed.

Fed up with people as good as telling her to her face that she was a Charm-free Zone, Bonny seized the opportunity to stick out her tongue, dig her thumbs in her ears, and waggle her fingers.

The lift doors opened again, and the man stared.

'I was quite wrong,' he said before they slid closed again properly. 'You were quite right. This is quite obviously the floor you need.'

♥ 11 ♥

All along the corridor were photographs of dolls. All sorts of dolls, from innocent blue-eyed china dolls to mischievous dark-eyed dolls. But all had shiny eyes with curly lashes, and clouds of perfect hair, and pearly teeth behind their painted, triumphant smiles. They all had names as well, printed beneath their pictures. Miss Rosebud, one was called. Miss Sweet Caroline was another. Little Miss Cute Candy hung between Princess Royale and Our Million Dollar Baby. And Miss Stardust even had a wand to match her glittery frock.

Miss Treasure   Miss Rosebud

Along the corridor came the tea boy, pushing his trolley. 'Are you lost?' he asked Bonny.

'No. I just stopped to look.'

'Choosing your favourite?'

Bonny stared at him coolly. 'I don't think so. I'm a bit old for dollies.'

The tea boy nodded at the pictures. 'Never too old to look like a twink.'

Bonny took a closer look at Miss Cute Candy. 'Are you *serious*? Are you telling me she's *real*?'

Princess Royale   Miss Cute Candy

'*Real*?' said the tea boy. 'She's a tiger, that one. She just this minute bit my head off for running a trolley wheel over one of her diamanté shoes.'

'What's diamanté?'

'Don't ask me,' he shrugged. 'That's what she called it when she threw her little tantrum.'

'Where is she now?' asked Bonny, a little nervously.

'Where do you think?' said the tea boy. 'She's behind that door with the others, spending the day in Charm School.'

Bonny was horrified. 'It didn't say!' she wailed. 'It didn't say anything on the pink sheet about dressing up like dollies!'

The tea boy shrugged. 'So? It doesn't say anything on the Woodwork I sheet about needing sticking plasters. Or on the Practical Parenting sheet about bringing your aspirins.'

'It's going to be *awful*, isn't it?' Bonny said.

'It's going to be *worse* than awful,' said the tea boy. 'It's always awful. But usually on Saturdays it's just Mrs Opalene's Charm School girls. They're bad enough. But on the one day a year she does the Curls and Purls

Show, we get a flood of dippy twinks from The Little Miss Pretty Circle. So it's *worse*.'

'The Little Miss Pretty Circle?' (It didn't just sound *worse*. It sounded *frightful*.)

He nodded at the photos on the walls. 'You'll see,' he warned her. 'Just go in and see.'

Bonny pushed open the door, and peeped inside. A dozen girls her age were sitting on chairs facing a little stage. Their backs were straight. Their hands were folded in their laps. And they were listening.

Up on the stage, a large, round, glittering lady strolled up and down.

'You're all *Stars*,' she was telling them. 'Every one of you. But when you come up on this stage, you're going to be *Superstars*!'

Bonny slid in the room and closed the door behind her. Nobody turned to look.

'All day I want to see your Prettiest Eyes and your Prettiest Smiles!'

Bonny took a seat on a chair in the back row, and nobody noticed.

'All day,' said the glittering lady, 'I shall be watching you. And do you know what I'm expecting to see?'

'Yes, Mrs Opalene,' chirruped a dozen little voices, quite drowning out Bonny's baffled, 'No.'

'I am expecting to see you walk as if you were on the brink of dancing.'

'Yes, Mrs Opalene.'

Mrs Opalene lifted a hand to her ear. 'And all day long I shall be listening. And do you know what I'm expecting to hear?'

'Yes, Mrs Opalene,' chirruped everyone except Bonny.

'I am expecting to hear you all talking as if you were about to burst into song.'

'Yes, Mrs Opalene.' Nobody sniggered. Nobody made a face. Nobody even turned to look at the person next to them.

'And when you're singing,' said Mrs Opalene. 'What am I expecting?'

'To hear an angel trying to get it absolutely right,' came the reply.

'And when you dance?'

'To be dazzled by our delicate footwork.'

'That's right. Lovely!' She clapped her hands together. Her rings flashed. 'So now we'll just go ahead and do everything we usually do on Saturday mornings in Charm School. But in the afternoon we'll have our special Curls and Purls Show.' Her eyes shone with excitement. 'And, just before you go home, we'll have The Crowning of The Supreme Queen, who gets to choose her very own pretty name to wear all year. And haven't we had some lovely ones!' She pressed her hands together, remembering. 'Miss Perfect Pearl! Miss Treasure! Dazzling Miss Daisy! Miss Sparkling Sue ...'

All round, everyone was clapping delightedly, except for Bonny, who sat with her head in her hands, even more sure now that she was in the wrong place, at the wrong time, with the wrong people. Should she get up and run? But there was something about the rising chatter round her, like sparrows squabbling on a fence, that made her feel even more homesick for her old friends.

So she'd give it a go. Someone would have to speak to her some time, after all. And maybe, even in this unlikely cluster of goody-two-shoes, she might find some company to keep her going through the long, lonely summer, till she could make some proper, sensible friends in her new school.

So when Mrs Opalene told everyone to take a little break while she set out her table for Beauty Tips, Bonny looked up. And when a girl she recognized from the photographs on the wall outside sailed past her, flashing a sparkling smile, Bonny said to her hopefully, 'Hello, Rosebud.'

The pretty vision twirled around. 'Who said that?'

'I did.'

'Why?'

Bonny stared. 'Because I don't know anyone here,' she said. 'And you just smiled at me.'

'I didn't smile at you,' the pretty vision snapped. 'I was just practising being *charming*.'

And off she went.

Rude, horrid *baggage*, thought Bonny. But it didn't seem fair to judge the whole lot of them by one bad-mannered, haughty girl. So when the one that Bonny recognized as Miss Sweet Caroline strolled over towards her, smiling, Bonny tried again.

'Hi, Caroline.'

The smile vanished instantly. The eyes flashed sparks of fire. And Miss Sweet Caroline said to Bonny, 'You say that again, and I'll stick your head in a holly bush.'

She swung on the heel of her shiny satin shoe, and stalked off, scowling. Bonny stared after her, astonished, until another of the girls came up behind. Though her hair was even longer and glossier than on the photograph outside, Bonny could tell it was Miss Stardust.

'Brilliant!' she said to Bonny. 'You certainly showed her!'

Bonny was baffled. All that she'd done to Miss Sweet Caroline was say hello.

'Showed who?' she asked.

'Silly old Sarajane.' Miss Stardust nodded after Miss Sweet Caroline. 'That was a smart way to remind her of the last time she won anything – about a million years ago! And she certainly needn't expect to win the glistering tiara today.'

'What glistering tiara?'

Miss Stardust waggled her pretty head from side to side in impatience.

'Why, the glistering tiara of Miss Supreme Queen, of course. Weren't you even *listening*?'

Suddenly Bonny couldn't even see her. A cloud of candy-floss hair had stepped between them. 'You can't be *Miss* Supreme Queen,' it corrected Miss Stardust officiously. 'You'd have to be "Your Highness, The Supreme Queen".'

'Well, thank you so very much, Cristalle,' snarled Miss Stardust. 'For wasting a whole corner of my brain by filling it up with something I don't need to know.'

'No,' snapped back Cristalle. 'I suppose you don't, Angelica, since you have absolutely no chance of winning it.'

Like Sarajane, she stalked off, just in time to pretend not to have heard Miss Stardust's cross-patchy hiss of, 'Neither have you!'

Bonny stared. Were they *all* horrid? Why had she thought they were like sparrows squabbling merrily on a fence? These girls were more like vultures, all hovering unpleasantly over the next glistering tiara to be won.

'Tell me,' she said to Angelica. 'Do you only get a photo on the wall outside if you're the winner?'

'That's right.'

'And, if you lose, do you have to wait a whole year to try again?'

'Yes,' said Angelica. 'And, if you win, you're crowned for the whole year.' Coughing politely, she modestly inspected her perfect finger-nails.

Bonny took the hint.

'So are you still Miss Stardust?'

'Yes, I am,' said Angelica firmly. 'I am Miss Stardust until four o'clock this afternoon. That gives me six hours, three minutes and—' She glanced at her watch. 'Fifteen seconds.'

Either she was a whizz at maths, thought Bonny, or she kept track by the second. Still trying to be friendly, she said to Angelica, 'But you might win again.'

Somehow, Angelica suddenly looked horribly anxious, and Bonny found herself adding hastily, in order to comfort her, 'Not that it matters. After all, winning isn't all that important.'

Angelica gasped. Her mouth dropped open and her eyes travelled up and down Bonny as if she were inspecting her properly for the first time: hair, face and clothing. She looked confused. 'Why are you here anyway?' she asked curiously after a moment. 'You've never come before. And look at you! You obviously haven't fallen to earth from Planet Fashion.'

Bonny couldn't help staring. If one of her old friends had said something like that, she would have thought that they were trying to be horrible. After all, it was the rudest thing that anyone had said to her in quite a while. But Miss Stardust somehow said it as if she were making a simple judgement of the facts, like 'Your eyes

are more blue than green', or, 'It's really too wet for a picnic.'

And it was the truth. No way round that. There's nothing amazing about a pair of blue jeans and a faded shirt, and plain blue canvas sneakers. So Bonny was about to explain about her mother and the bookkeeping, and Dad stuck in the lay-by, and being new in town, when up sailed Miss Cute Candy, walking for all the world as if she were on the brink of dancing, pointing her pretty, sparkling shoes like a ballerina fairy, and waving her fingers elegantly in the air, as if the polish on her nails were still not dry.

'Who's this?' she demanded of Angelica, staring at Bonny.

'How should I know?' Angelica responded petulantly. 'I only just met her.' She turned away, making it clear that the last thing she wanted was to be caught up in conversation with Miss Cute Candy. Why were they all so scratchy with one another, Bonny wondered. And then she realized. If the whole day was a sort of competition, and they were rivals, then each time they even looked at one another, all they would see would be one more person who might snatch away that delectable, desirable, glistering tiara. What tiny-minded *pains* they were clearly going to be, even for a few short hours.

Now Miss Cute Candy was eyeing Bonny up and down.

'Where's all your stuff?'

'I haven't got any.'

'What, none? No make-up? Nothing for your nails? No stuff to fix your hair?'

Poor Bonny's heart was sinking. 'No. None of that.'

'Well, what about music tapes for your routine, and instructions for the lighting?'

'I haven't got those, either.'

Miss Cute Candy stared. 'Well, surely you've brought a gown for the catwalk parade, and an outfit for your song-and-dance routine?'

'No. No, I haven't.'

'I don't see why you're even here,' said Miss Cute Candy. 'What's the point of showing up if all you're going to be is One Big Nothing?'

It was another really rude remark, though Bonny could tell that, just like Miss Stardust, she wasn't trying to be nasty; she was just curious. But, even so, the idea of being One Big Nothing wasn't nice. It was quite obvious that showing up at Charm School without a pile of the right stuff was just about as hopeless as turning up at Practical Parenting without a baby. But what was so special about dressing up? These girls were all swanning about as if just looking your prettiest gave you the right to act as if other people were just grease spots on the carpet. You'd have a whole lot more right to strut around, Bonny thought sourly, if you could actually do something clever.

Do something clever ... Her brain was ticking over fast now. She'd have a horrible day if she let anybody know that she was here for Charm School, that was for sure. They'd already spotted her for a total loser. Even the man who stepped in the lift had thought she must be wandering around on the wrong floor, unless she had come to help someone called Maura with—

Bonny stared down at Miss Cute Candy's beautiful twinkling dancing shoes, and her own plain old sneakers. And in one brilliant diamanté flash came inspiration.

'I'm not here for the same reasons you are. I'm only here to give a hand with the sound and the lighting.'

'Oh, you're just one of Maura's little helpers!' Miss Cute Candy didn't just manage to make this sound as if she found it a much more likely idea than Bonny on a catwalk. In her keenness to let Bonny know exactly what she wanted in the lighting line, she spoke as if Bonny were some little garden gnome brought to life, just for the day, to be useful. 'Now look here, quick!' Grabbing Bonny's arm, she spun her round to face the mirror that ran the whole length of the wall. 'See all those horrible lumps? Well, what I want you to do is fix up the lighting so—'

'What horrible lumps?' asked Bonny, mystified.

'Those!' Miss Cute Candy said, pointing.

So Bonny looked again. All she could see in the mirror was herself, the flat grey wall behind, and Miss Cute Candy in her silky yellow dress and diamanté slippers, like an exotic spring flower rising, willowy and graceful, from a spangled pool.

'I can't see any lumps.'

Miss Cute Candy patted at the folds of her skirt.

'These,' she said. 'The lumps on these great ugly tree stumps.'

'Are you talking about your legs?'

'Legs!' scoffed Miss Cute Candy. 'They're so huge, they're more like pillars in a multi-storey car park!'

Was she serious? One minute, she'd been lording it over Bonny as if she were Miss World and Bonny were some little goblin. And the next minute, she was panicking about the size of her legs.

And really panicking. This was no joke. There was a tremble in her voice, Bonny could tell. And she was close to tears.

Bonny suddenly felt sorry for her, just the same way she'd felt sorry for Angelica for worrying about winning.

'Don't be so silly,' she tried to comfort her. 'You look—'

But Miss Cute Candy was too upset even to listen. 'I look horrible. Horrible! I'm fat and hideous. My nails are a sight. My hands would look more delicate stuffed inside oven gloves. I've got the worst legs in the world. My stomach sticks out like a pig's belly. My hair's turned to straw. I'm ugly, ugly, ugly.' She made a face at herself in the mirror. 'Ugly!' she jeered again. 'I'm a horrible little gnome and my clothes look like jumble.'

'Jumble?' This was beyond ridiculous. 'How can you say that your clothes look like jumble? That dress looks to me as if it comes from one of the smartest shops in town. And those sparkly slippers must have cost a *fortune*!'

But Miss Cute Candy was still staring despairingly into the huge wide mirror.

'It's not the clothes. They're all right, I suppose. It's what they look like on me. They do look like jumble. I bulge out all over, I'm so fat.' She started beating at her thighs with bunched-up fists. 'Fat, fat, fat! That's what I am. Fat!'

Bonny was mystified. Was this one of the little tantrums the tea boy had mentioned when he called Miss Cute Candy a tiger? But she didn't seem at all tigerish to Bonny. She seemed *desperate*. So maybe Bonny should rush down to Bookkeeping (Advanced) and fetch her mother, who could come up and say what she always said to Bonny when she was being silly about her hair, or her face, or the shape of her body.

Or Bonny could just try saying it herself.

'Don't be so soft. You know you're beautiful.'

'I am not! I am *not*!'

But how could Bonny go on and say the next bit? How could you say to someone whom you hardly knew, 'Well, you are to *me*! And even if you weren't, I wouldn't care. Even if you were the worst-looking person in the world, with a face like a squashed tomato and a body like a car wreck, I'd still love you so much I could burst, and so will everyone who ever gets to know you.'?

You can't make a speech like that to someone you've only just met, even if you know it backwards. And Bonny did. She'd heard her mother saying it a thousand times. She'd heard it when she came home from nursery school crying because Robert said she had a face like his toy bath duck. She'd heard it after she won the painting prize, and Estelle was jealous and whispered to everyone that Bonny looked like a maggot. She heard it from her mother over and over the year she was in Mrs Hamilton's class, because Mrs Hamilton never bothered to stop people being mean to one another, and Flora and her gang picked on all the other girls, giggling in corners, and saying horrible things about their hair and their clothes and their faces. And, now she thought about it, she'd heard it only a few weeks ago, when she came home from her music lesson.

'What's up with you?' her mum had said. 'You look like a wet afternoon in Wolverhampton. What's the matter?'

'I'm all right.'

'Bad lesson?'

Bonny shook her head. 'It was all right.'

'Perhaps you're not feeling well.'

'I'm all right.'

She'd tried to get away to her bedroom, but Mum had caught her as she rushed past, and turned her round to look at her.

'Well, *something*'s not all right,' she'd said. 'Or you wouldn't be looking as if you're about to spill teardrops on my freshly mopped floor.'

And Bonny had burst into noisy sobs, and told her all about Mr Spicer poking his head out of the teaching room, and saying, 'You're a big beefy girl. Be an angel, and carry this cello along to the hall for me.'

'Yes …?'

Mum was still waiting, Bonny could tell.

'That's it!' she wailed. 'He called me a big beefy girl!'

'He meant strong enough to carry a cello.'

'*Beefy*, he said!'

And Mum had had to swivel her round and point her at the mirror. 'Look,' she said. 'See that stranger? Is she so big that people step off the pavement when she comes along?'

'No,' Bonny said sullenly.

'Do people point at her? Or even stare?'

'No,' Bonny admitted unwillingly.

'Listen,' said Mum. And then she'd made the exact same speech she'd been making since Bonny was four, finishing up, as usual: 'You may not be perfect, but you're perfectly normal. And only dolls are perfect.'

Well, Bonny could at least say that to Miss Cute Candy. 'Only dolls are perfect.'

Miss Cute Candy rolled her eyes. 'Oh, really? Well, what about all those photos of the Curls and Purls Girls on the wall outside?'

The Curls and Purls Girls! The very sound of it made Bonny want to stick her fingers down her throat. 'Oh, *please!*' she said. 'Little Miss Airhead! Sweet Miss Empty-Brain! It's out of the Ark, this idea of dressing up for the afternoon as Miss Baby Perfect, with a frozen dolly smile and concrete sprayed hair. Who cares which one of the Little Miss Dippy Circle—'

'Little Miss *Pretty* Circle,' Miss Cute Candy corrected her sharply. 'Get it *right*.'

'Why? Are you in it?'

'I'm not just *in* it,' Miss Cute Candy said. 'I'm Cindy-Lou Brown, the secretary! And you needn't be rude about it. It's been going longer than any club you're in, I'll bet. My older sisters were both in it. And so was my mother. And so were both my aunties. One of them was even Miss Sparkling Sue.'

'But that's what I'm *saying*,' said Bonny. 'Who wants to worry about who wins some silly competition that was started way back when dinosaurs were roaming the earth, and Mrs Opalene was young? It doesn't have anything to do with real people living real lives. I bet there's no-one, even in this room, who could look perfect all day every day. Because, like I told you, only *dolls* are perfect.'

'Well, that's just where you're *wrong*!' snapped Cindy-Lou. Irritation fought with envy, and won. 'Because *Amethyst*'s perfect. *And* she's not just good at winning practically every Little Miss Pretty Circle competition. She's also one of Mrs Opalene's pets in Charm School as well.'

'Which one is Amethyst?' Bonny asked curiously.

Cindy-Lou pointed to where a girl with a shimmering waterfall of hair was putting chairs in a circle round a sign that said, in bright gold lettering:

MRS OPALENE'S HANDY HELPING HINTS

'That's her. She's getting ready for the Beauty and Grooming tips.'

'Why would she bother with those,' Bonny tried to catch Cindy-Lou out, 'if she's already perfect?'

'You've got to keep up,' Cindy-Lou told Bonny sternly. 'Fashions and styles keep changing so people who aren't paying attention get left behind. That's why some of the girls from our Little Miss Pretty Circle come here to Mrs Opalene's Charm School every Saturday, and not just for her big Curls and Purls Competition. Mrs Opalene's really good at giving people all those special little tips that make the world of difference.'

The world of difference! Bonny stared. But just at that moment, as if to show how very keen she was not to miss any of these quite amazing tips, Cindy-Lou abandoned Bonny and rushed off to take her place in Amethyst's perfect circle of chairs even before Mrs Opalene had clapped her hands for attention.

'Girlies! Girlies, it's Beauty Tip time! Now I'm starting today with a small variation on that old idea of bleaching your elbows by sticking them in two halves of squeezed lemon.'

Bleaching your *elbows*? Bonny crept closer, fascinated.

Mrs Opalene waved a stern finger round the circle of girls who had hurried to their seats and pulled out their notebooks and pens. 'And I hope I don't have to remind anyone here that, *contrary* to what we read in some cheap and nasty little magazines, we don't use up our leftover lemon juice in the last clear rinse of our hair wash. And why not, Amethyst?'

Amethyst flicked her hair shyly. 'Because it strips it of the natural oils?'

'That's right, dear.'

Amethyst flicked her hair again, pleased.

'*Well*,' said Mrs Opalene, twinkling with enthusiasm. 'Some *very* clever person has worked out that, while you're sitting with your elbows in your lemon halves, you could be doing something inordinately useful at the same time.'

She gazed around at them. 'Can anybody guess what that might be?'

It seemed an easy enough question. 'Reading a good book?' suggested Bonny.

Mrs Opalene waved a beringed hand. 'Do try not to be silly, dear. This is seriou—' She broke off, inspecting Bonny properly for the first time. 'You look a little ...' She paused, puzzled, as she eyed this newcomer to her class up and down from plain old top to plain old toe. 'Dear, you don't seem quite ...' Again, she stopped, and peered even more closely. 'Are you *supposed* to be here?'

'Yes,' Bonny said, fingering the ticket in her pocket. She was about to explain when Cindy-Lou called out from her side of the circle.

'She's here to help Maura with the sound and the lighting.'

At once, she was the most popular person in the universe and everyone was calling out.

'Oh, please! May I just tell you something?'

'I have to explain to you exactly what I need.'

'Listen, there's a bit in my music where—'

'When Maura gets to the lighting for my bit—'

'You see, I have this problem with—'

'Girls! Girls!' Mrs Opalene clapped to hush them. 'Everyone will get their turn to visit the back room.' She turned back to Bonny. 'Well, dear,' she said. 'You do look awfully young to be dealing with expensive equipment. But I suppose if Maura thinks it's all right—' She gazed around. 'Has anyone seen Maura this morning?'

Most of the faces looked blank, though one framed by a mass of midnight blue ribbons began to crease, as if some worrying, half-remembered message was drifting to mind.

'Don't screw your face up, dear,' Mrs Opalene reproved her. 'It will only encourage early wrinkling.' And then, as if this reminded her of all she had to get through that morning, she impatiently waved Bonny out of the circle. 'All right, dear. Off you go.'

And Bonny, equally reminded of all she wanted to miss, sprang to her feet, delighted at this chance to flee from all their drippy lectures about bleached elbows and natural hair oils. The tea boy was right. They were ridiculous, perched in a circle on their little chairs, like fairies waiting for some wonderland party.

But Miss Stardust had jumped to her feet as well.

'Oh, please let me go with her,' she begged Mrs Opalene. 'Just so I can explain about my flashing lights.'

'Not yet, dear, because I'm sure Miss—'

She stopped and peered at Bonny, waiting for a name.

'"Sparky",' bossy Cristalle insisted, nodding her puffy hair. 'You always call electricians "Sparky". It's a theatre rule.'

'*Miss* Sparky,' reproved Mrs Opalene. 'I'm sure we don't *ever* want to forget our manners.' She turned back to Bonny, still peering, and started rooting in her bag. Bonny was sure that she was searching for her spectacles, and when she put them on she'd see at once that, even for somebody's helper, Bonny was terribly young – no older than everyone round her.

But then Miss Stardust started up again. 'About my flashing lights—'

'No!' said Mrs Opalene. 'Right now we're busy with our Handy Helping Hints. And since no-one's seen Maura yet, Miss Sparky had better start getting everything set up and ready for our rehearsals for the Curls and Purls Show.'

Bonny was horrified. What she'd been hoping to do was sneak away to find her mother. Vanish and never come back. Mum might have given her that stern look over her spectacles, and ordered her back with a lecture on not wasting money – warmly applauded, probably, Bonny thought bitterly, by all the other people in Bookkeeping (Advanced). But even then she could have spent the day lurking in some cupboard, out of sight.

But now they were expecting her to walk the other way – to the door at the back of the room. And then start up lights and music by herself! She was no expert in anything like that. She knew how to use her own music equipment, of course. And she was as good as anyone else at flicking on a light switch. But running the sound and lighting for the rehearsals for a Curls and Purls Show – even making things flash for Miss Stardust – well, that was different.

Better confess that she was really here, like all the rest, to listen to the Handy Hints.

But just at that moment Mrs Opalene spoke up again.

'So, dears. Back to all this time we have to spare, sitting with our elbows in our lemons. What are we going to do with it? Well, one quite *brilliant* idea is to make sure our feet are busy soaking in a bucket of perfumed water to soften all that nasty hard skin that gathers at the back of our poor heels!'

Bonny looked round. No-one was sniggering. No-one was rolling their eyes. No-one was even making a face of mock astonishment. They were all diligently taking notes.

Bonny turned round and set off determinedly for the back room.

Better Miss Sparky than Miss Twink.

CHAPTER TWO

The small back room looked like the cockpit of an airplane. There were switches everywhere. Switches to the right of her, switches to the left, and switches on the panel under the glass window through which she could see Mrs Opalene lecturing everyone on how to cope with all that nasty hard skin at the back of their heels.

And watching her.

Should she just sit there pretending? When Maura turned up, she could just say that she'd been looking for a phone or some water, and slip away.

Or should she have a go? After all, Maura might be very late. Or she might even have forgotten she was supposed to be there at all.

Bonny looked up. There on the panel right above her head was one big red master switch, labelled POWER.

No point in being chicken, Bonny thought. She flicked it down. At once, a hundred lights began to blink at her, red, white and green.

'Oh, excellent!' she breathed. 'Oh, yes! That's power!'

STORM ○
Tempest ○
SNOW ⇨
Thunder ○
Sleet ○
Fog ○
Bit of drizzle ○
Downpour ○
Cats & dogs ○
Very windy ○
Lightning ⇨

Taking the swivel seat, she whirled around. Best to get going. She might as well start with the panel in front of her. Just like any kitchen or toolshed, the things that were closest were probably the most useful.

Choosing a switch, she slid it gently up its track. Instantly, from the loudspeaker on the wall behind, she heard Mrs Opalene's voice, clear as a bell.

'So I certainly hope I don't have to remind anyone here—'

Bonny slid up the next switch. Mrs Opalene's voice turned deep and resonant. Almost booming.

'—that they should never, *ever* miss the chance of putting slices of fresh cucumber—'

Bonny slid the switch down again and pushed up the one on the other side. The voice went high and tinny.

'—on their eyelids. It isn't just refreshing—'

So that was the bass and the treble sorted out. Bonny switched Mrs Opalene's voice back to normal.

'—it also makes the *world* of difference.'

For heaven's sake! thought Bonny. There it was again, that silly claim, 'It makes the world of difference'. What was the matter with them all? Did they have maggots for brains? When did you ever bump into someone on the street, and think, Oh, look at those eyes! She must have been lying under cucumber slices? Distracted as she was by all the switches she was pushing up and down, still Bonny couldn't help muttering sarcastically, 'Oh, yes! Spit in my eye and then tell me it's raining!'

They heard it in there, she could tell. Everyone's face swivelled to stare at her through the huge glass window.

'Sorry!' called Bonny, switching off the blinking light labelled SOUND OUT.

She left SOUND IN still blinking.

So, for all the embarrassment, at least that was one more of Maura's little tricks under her belt. She turned to the buttons beside her. The first ones she pressed lit up the stage in dazzling circles.

'Spotlights!'

She tried more. This time, the whole front apron of the stage was bathed in a silver glow.

'Floodlights,' muttered Bonny.

She pressed a few more buttons and watched as huge, spotty red and green explosions bounced off the drapes on each side of the stage. On the backcloth behind, a waterfall appeared from nowhere, rippling down to a pool of foaming water.

'Special effects!'

She looked down. Inside the boxes at her feet were discs of every colour. And stencils, too. Some were cut into shapes she recognized, like windows or trees, and others were just cut into the strangest patterns. She picked out two and stared at them, trying to imagine what they would look like cast up on the back of the stage, lit up and enormous.

'Oh, yes! This one's a snowstorm! And this one is clouds.'

She was just peering through the next one – creepy forest branches? – when she was startled by a whisper from a loudspeaker overhead.

'Oh, no! Oh, no!' The voice was aghast. 'I ate it! I just ate it!'

Bonny spun round to look through the glass. Beside one of the microphones she must have left switched on, there were two latecomers she hadn't noticed. They'd stopped to stare at one another in the middle of changing their shoes.

'Oh, Cooki! You didn't!'

'I did, Lulu! One minute it was in my hand, and the next it was gone. I must have eaten it. I *must*.'

Poor thing! thought Bonny, remembering all too clearly how she'd felt when Herbie Stott slid a dead ant into the icing on her fairy cake and didn't tell her till she'd finished it. And when she'd gone to take the second bite of that apple Granny gave her, and saw the maggot hole – one swallow too late.

Lulu was looking horrified. 'You never ate the whole thing. Not *the whole thing*.'

'I must have, without noticing.'

♥ 47 ♥

'Cooki, how *could* you? They're *enormous*. How could you not even notice you were gobbling a whole biscuit?'

'I don't know! I don't know!' Cooki was almost in tears.

Bonny peered through the glass at this strange pair. A biscuit? How could you possibly get so upset about eating a biscuit? And if you went round acting as if scoffing one miserable biscuit was just about as terrible as eating your own granny, then how could you stand to have a name like Cooki? It would drive you mad.

She could flick on the SOUND OUT switch, and ask. But Mrs Opalene was on to yet another handy hint.

'So we never waste time at a bus stop! Wherever we are, it's exercise, exercise! We could be pulling in our tummy muscles. We could be swirling our ankles round to keep them trim. We could even be doing little knee bends to work on those flabby thighs—'

Bonny was baffled. None of the girls in the circle had thighs that looked any thicker than toast, and even Mrs Opalene was wearing such a gorgeous floaty skirt that no-one with a brain worth waking in the morning would waste time wondering about the legs it hid. Cupping her chin in her hands, Bonny gazed out through the glass. 'Batty!' she muttered to herself, shaking her head. 'Totally batty, the whole lot of them.'

She heard a voice behind her. 'Well, that's what happens to people who won't eat properly. First they waste away. Then they go mad.'

Bonny spun round. It was the tea boy again. He'd slid in silently and was putting two biscuits on a plate down on a ledge.

'Maura's mid-morning snack,' he said, pointing. 'Shall I leave you a couple as well, or are you—?'

'Oh, goody!' Bonny was already stretching out for the packet he was offering.

'Well, look at you!' the tea boy said admiringly. 'Straight in the trough! I can see you won't last all that long up here on Planet Snack-on-Air.'

Bonny couldn't help grinning. It wasn't the most polite thing to say – straight in the trough! – but it did prove to her that there was at least one other person in the world who thought this place was Crazy Club.

'Who are you?'

'I'm Toby. Being the tea boy is my Saturday job.' He sighed. 'Though I hate it so much I could practically *die*.'

'Why do you do it, then?' Bonny asked curiously.

'For the money, of course. I'm saving for a new violin.' He sighed again, even more heavily. 'Though sometimes I'm not sure it's worth it, trailing up and down these corridors all day just to make the music I play sound a little bit better.'

'It can't be too bad,' Bonny pointed out. 'Just dishing out the tea and biscuits.'

'And wisdom,' Toby pointed out. 'Don't forget wisdom. I can dish that out, too.'

Bonny laughed, pointing through the glass. 'If you're so wise,' she said, 'then tell me this. What's wrong with all of them? Why are they all the way they are?'

'I blame Mrs Opalene,' said Toby. 'Her words fly in one ear, and all their brains fly out the other.'

They both broke off to listen.

'As good as poison!' Mrs Opalene was warning everyone. 'Just fat and chemicals in fancy wrappers!'

'What is she on about now?'

'Possibly the cheaper range of my biscuits,' Toby admitted. 'Or sweets and crisps. She's got a bit of a thing about them.'

'That's not so odd. My mum and dad go on about them all the time.'

'Oh, everyone gets that,' said Toby. 'But Mrs Opalene acts as if one sweetie will blacken and rot your insides, and one little chocolate bar will make you swell till you explode.'

'And Lulu and Cooki act as if they believe her.'

'They all do.'

'I don't know why,' said Bonny. 'After all, Mrs Opalene's not exactly a beanpole herself. And she looks healthy enough.'

'Yes,' Toby agreed. 'Plump and cosy-looking.

And it suits her. So why she's so determined to starve these poor followers of hers into staircase spindles, I really don't know. But she never lets up. She's like some mad general, always going on about the Great Food War. You listen.'

He switched Mrs Opalene's voice up till it filled the room.

'So,' boomed the exultant tones. 'We're going to make two precious lists. On one, we're going to put all our Food Friends.' Mrs Opalene beamed. 'All those Handy Little Helpers to Happy Health. Like—?'

She waited.

'Raw vegetables!'

'Grilled fish!'

'Skimmed milk!'

They were all clapping in delight.

Mrs Opalene's face darkened now, and her voice went sombre. 'But on the other list, we're going to put all our Food Enemies. All those horrible, fatty, worthless—'

'Food Fiends!'

Some of them were even hissing.

'Chips!'

'Chocolate!'

'Fry-ups!'

'Sweet drinks!'

'Ice cream!'

And, in a wail of misery from Cooki, 'And horrible sneaky biscuits that creep up on you when you're not even looking, and practically *throw* themselves into your mouth.'

Bonny turned to the tea boy. 'I hope it's not catching.'

He picked up the empty biscuit plate. 'It looks as if you've been safe enough so far.'

'Did I eat Maura's as well? I am sorry,' Bonny said. 'I didn't notice.'

'That's because you're not yet under the spell. So just be careful. Block your ears till I come round again.'

He left to go back to his trolley just as Mrs Opalene changed tack.

'And now, dears,' Bonny heard her saying. 'We're going to spend a bit of time practising our sitting.'

Practising sitting! Bonny rolled her eyes. She hadn't practised sitting since the last time she fell off her potty, and she wasn't going to start again now. Switching Mrs Opalene's voice down to a soft burble, she turned to the nearest big floor lamp and tried

♥ 53 ♥

to work out which of the knobs made the beam of light blur and sharpen, and which faded it out slowly or snapped it off fast. She'd just learned how to slide the colour sheets in front of the light beam when the door flew open. It was the girl whose hair was a mass of midnight blue ribbons. From her hand trailed a white shawl spangled with crystals like sunlight glittering on a heap of snow.

Coolly, she leaned against the doorway.

'Is that seat you're on comfy enough?' she asked, pointing at Bonny's swivel chair.

'Yes, thank you,' Bonny said, pleased someone cared. 'Very comfy.'

'It's not too grubby?'

'No.'

'There aren't grease spots all over it?' said the girl, concerned.

'No, really. It's fine.'

'What about the draught? Is it messing up your hair?'

'No, I don't think so.'

'Right,' said the girl. 'Hotch off, then. I'll sit there.'

Resisting the urge to shove this pushy visitor over backwards, Bonny said frostily, 'Are these the sort of manners you've learned in Charm School? Because, if they are, maybe your mother should ask for her money back.'

'And maybe yours should send you back where you came from.'

'Oh, yes?' challenged Bonny. 'And where's that?'

'Well, from the look of you,' the girl said, 'I'd say, The Land of No Style.'

'Better,' said Bonny icily, 'than crawling here from The Land of No Manners.'

The girl was pointing now. 'You realize the pattern on that blouse looks like a skin disease?'

'You obviously missed the class called Secrets of Flattery.'

'That mop on the top of your head doesn't even look like hair.'

'And no-one could possibly mistake you for a nice person.'

The girl let rip now. 'Oh, go fry your face!'

'Nosebleed!' snapped Bonny.

'Squirrelbrain!'

'Superbrat!'

'Oh, wonderful!' Suddenly, to Bonny's astonishment, the girl flung her arms wide, shut her eyes tight, and spun round merrily on her toes. 'Oh, brilliant! That feels a whole lot better!' Opening her eyes again, she stuck out her hand and gave Bonny a huge friendly smile. 'Hi,' she said. 'Sorry about all that. But, really, it's not easy to go round being charming all day. Sometimes you find you have to run away for a few minutes to let off steam.'

'What?' Bonny said, baffled. 'Didn't you mean any of it?'

'Well, no. Not really,' said the girl. 'I mean,

I quite like your blouse. And your hair looks perfectly normal.' She looked a little wistful. 'I suppose I wasn't making it up about wanting to sit in the chair, though. I wouldn't mind a little go on that. What's your swivelling record?'

'Four times round,' Bonny admitted, getting off it. 'Then it grinds to a halt.'

'Have you tried winding it right down to base before you start?'

'No,' Bonny said. 'I never thought.'

The girl tossed her glittering shawl onto the ledge, out of the way, and together they peered under the chair. 'No,' she said sadly after a moment. 'See? It's got a sort of lock on it, to stop the seat base flying off the chassis.'

'You seem to know an awful lot about swivel chairs.'

'I know a lot about *every* sort of chair. Here in Charm School we spend an awful lot of time just sitting waiting.'

'And then you go home to stick your elbows in lemon halves and sit and wait some more,' Bonny couldn't help pointing out.

'Only because it really works!' In her enthusiasm to twist her elbows round to show Bonny just how nicely they were bleached, the newcomer accidentally knocked a switch that set Mrs Opalene's voice reverberating over and over through the tiny room.

'Oh, brilliant!' said Bonny. 'You've found the echo for me!'

Both of them listened. Through all the copycat repeats bouncing from the walls as they faded, they could still make out what Mrs Opalene was saying.

'You are all beautiful! You owe it to the world to smile, smile, smile!'

Smile! Smile! the walls reminded them. *Smile! Smile! Smile! Smile!*

'I'd better get back.' On hearing Mrs Opalene's voice, Bonny's beribboned visitor had lifted her head and straightened her back, and begun to point out her toes as if she were on the brink of dancing. Was this what Toby meant about falling under the spell, Bonny suddenly wondered. And she was sorry, because, until that moment, she'd really been getting to like her cheerful new visitor. Quickly, before losing her to Mrs Opalene completely, she switched the voice burbling out of the loudspeaker down to softer than soft, and said, 'Oh, please don't go. Not till you've told me your name.'

'I'm Araminta,' the girl said in a voice so lilting it sounded as if she were about to burst into song. 'But all my friends call me Minty.'

'*Minty?*'

The girl's eyes widened. 'Is there something wrong?'

'No.' Bonny was embarrassed. 'I was just wondering why so many of you seem to be named after your enemies.'

'Enemies?' The girl shook her head. 'I don't believe I have any enem—'

'Those Food Fiends,' Bonny interrupted to explain. 'Minty. Cooki. Candy. You're all named after things you're not supposed to eat.'

'I'm hardly going to be called Carrot, am I?' Araminta chortled. 'Or Celery. Or Cucumber.'

For the first time since she'd arrived in this strange new town, Bonny felt as if she were having the sort of conversation she used to have with her old friends. 'You could be called Lettuce,' she suggested. 'That's a name. Or—'

But Mrs Opalene's voice had raised itself above its own soft burbling. 'Araminta! I hope you're not wasting Miss Sparky's time in there. How long can it take to explain what you want for one little song and dance routine? Don't forget there are other girls waiting.'

Araminta leaned over the microphone on Bonny's panel. Bonny switched to Sound Out just long enough for her to coo, 'Coming, Mrs Opalene.' And when Araminta turned back, to Bonny's disappointment it was obvious that she didn't have any more time for friendly chatter. Her tone was now firm and businesslike.

'Now, listen. I'm going to be a dancing snowflake so I'll need a haze of glistening white with maybe a hint of blue to make it look even colder. And I'll need snowflaky light spangles swirling around me, to match the crystals twinkling on my shawl. But don't forget to keep my face in a warm spotlight or I'll look so awful everyone will die of fright.' She pointed through the glass. 'I'll go and stand where I'll be, and you do a lighting test.'

A lighting test! Bonny was horrified. She'd hardly worked out where anything was and how it worked, and now she was practically being examined in it! She'd be caught out at once. Firstly she'd look like an idiot. And then she'd almost certainly be frogmarched down to her mother in deep disgrace. Or, worse, sent back to the big room to fail at something even more difficult – being charming.

As casually as possible, she said to Araminta, 'I don't suppose you happen to remember what sort of lights and things worked best for you last time ...?'

'I wasn't a snowflake last time,' Araminta said. 'I was a cowgirl.' Then, sensing that under Bonny's careless shrug there was real disappointment, she added kindly, 'But Suki did sing a little Winter Frost Song the time before that. And if I remember rightly, Maura fixed things so that—'

She broke off and clapped her hand over her mouth, staring at Bonny. 'Oh, no! Maura! I *knew* there was something I was supposed to tell Mrs Opalene!'

Bonny's heart sank. 'Oh, no!' she wailed in turn. 'I bet you were supposed to tell Mrs Opalene that Maura can't come today to do the lighting and the sound.' She was about to add, 'And I'll be on my own here, all day,' but it sounded so terrifying, she couldn't even bear to say it.

'Oh, dear!' But was this Araminta looking guilty at forgetting a message even a toddler could have remembered without much trouble? No. She was halfway to giggling. 'Oh, I'm such a noodlebrain! It was the very last thing she said to me when I was helping her last time.'

Poor, desperate Bonny felt a glimmer of hope. 'Helping her?'

'Oh, yes.' Araminta waved at the boxes stacked across the floor. 'I always enjoyed helping Maura. I'm tidy by nature, you see. So I quite enjoy putting things away.'

Bonny could almost have hugged this cheerful, sparkling girl who might yet save her bacon. 'So do you know where everything is kept?'

'Most of it.'

'Show me!' challenged Bonny. 'Let's just pretend there's someone standing in the right place for a lighting test and show me how you would set things up.'

'I have a better idea,' said Araminta. 'Let's ask Pearl. She'll be happy to be our stand-in. Pearl loves getting out of Mrs Opalene's Handy Hints. She says they're—-' She stopped and giggled. 'No, I mustn't say it.'

'Mustn't say what?'

'What Pearl says about Handy Hints.'

'And what *does* Pearl say?'

Araminta spread her hands in merry wonder. 'She says she thinks some of them are a tiny bit boring.'

Bonny made a sour face. Her disappointment was intense. Anywhere else in the world, she would have longed to make friends with someone as sunny and exotic, someone so wonderfully irrepressible, as Araminta. And the two of them had been on the very edge of doing something really different and exciting – getting through the whole day without Mrs Opalene even guessing that Bonny wasn't the *real* Miss Sparky (or even a Miss Sparky at all). But now Araminta had reminded her that it was hopeless. Hopeless! What was the point of even dreaming of doing exciting things or making new friends in this stupid, stupid Charm School?

'Yes, Pearl's quite wrong,' she said. 'They're not a tiny bit boring at all. They're *enormously* boring, and quite *ridiculous*.'

'No, they're not!' Araminta sounded quite hurt and stung. 'Why, Serena's sister followed Mrs Opalene's handy hint about never sitting in front of the television without first dipping your hands in vegetable oil and wrapping them in clingfilm. And she got a job holding plates up to the sunlight in a washing-up advertisement.'

'Is that why you're here?' Bonny couldn't help teasing. 'So you can get to hold plates up to sunlight too?'

But Araminta missed the tone of sarcasm in her voice. She was too busy lifting her pretty little hands and shuddering. 'Don't be silly! I've got ugly great paws like giant soup plates!' It sounded so familiar. For just a moment, Bonny couldn't think why. And then she remembered Miss Cute Candy slapping at her perfectly normal legs, and calling them car park pillars.

Araminta tucked her hands away behind her back, out of sight, and said winsomely, 'But it would be nice to be *some* sort of model ...'

Bonny gazed out through the glass. 'I expect they all think that.'

'Not all of them.' Araminta pointed round the circle. 'Serena's here because she wants to be an actress, and she thinks looking nice and being charming will help her. And Lulu's here because her mother always wanted to be a catwalk star, but then she missed her big chance by getting married and having babies.

So she thought Lulu might like to have a go instead. And Sarajane's here because she's friends with Lulu and they go shopping after. And Cristalle's here because her dad is a top banker and he thinks that a charming, well-dressed secretary who does her hair nicely can get higher up in her job.'

'Maybe if she spent less time on her hair and more on her studies, she could get to be a top banker too. Then she could tell *him* what to wear,' Bonny said crossly.

But Araminta wasn't listening.

'And Esmeralda comes because her sister used to come. And Suki just comes to show off. And—'

'Show off? Show off what?'

'Anything. Everything. Whatever's new, Suki always somehow has it. And Mrs Opalene talks about it during the fashion tips. I expect she's doing that now, because that's Suki, pointing to her necklace thing, and I've never seen that before.'

Araminta turned up the sound on the speakers, so they could both listen.

'You see, dears,' Mrs Opalene was saying. 'As I keep telling everyone, it's so important to make sure you keep up to date. Take Suki's new pearl choker. Another girl might have been happy to dig any old double strand of pearls out of her jewellery case. But, Suki, dear, tell the others what you read in last week's issue of *Model Miss*.'

Araminta and Bonny watched Suki toss back her glistening mane of hair, and blush becomingly.

'It said that pearl chokers with only two strands are,' she shook her head in horror, '"*Totally Yesterday*".'

There was a little buzz around the circle.

'Really? I didn't know.'

'I heard that, too.'

'Oh, how upsetting! I've only just saved up and bought one!'

'It's horrid, isn't it?' Cooki was sympathising with the shocked Serena. 'But Suki's right. I read it too, in this month's *House of Style*. It said that two-strand chokers are "from Tiredsville" now, and the only thing to wear is three-strand chokers.'

Mrs Opalene clapped her hands to try to put a stop to the gossiping. 'So, go on, Suki. Tell everyone exactly what you did to find a three-strand choker for your dance on Saturday.'

Suki shrugged modestly. 'I went to forty different shops.'

'*Forty*?'

'Oh, Suki! That's amazing!'

The girls had taken to chattering again.

'Twenty-two is the most I've ever been to, looking for something special.'

'Sarajane and I went round thirty once, looking for the exact right plum suede boots. But we were together, and it took us a whole *week*.'

'But Suki did it all in one day. She must have been shattered afterwards.'

'Talk about Shop Till You Drop!'

Suki tilted her head and smiled modestly. 'Yes, I was tired. In fact, I was so tired, I fell asleep before the dancing even started.'

'Never mind. At least you *looked* right.'

'Oh, yes. I looked right. I checked before I left home, and I looked exactly like all the girls in this week's *Model Miss*.'

'There!' said Mrs Opalene. 'What an example for us all! Not ten shops. Not twenty. Not even thirty. Suki went to forty shops to get exactly what she wanted. And what do we call that, girls?'

Bonny could think of one answer. But a

quick sideways glance at Araminta's seraphically devoted face warned her to keep it to herself. Besides, everyone in the circle beyond the glass had started chanting.

'That's *dedication*, Mrs Opalene.'

'That's right, dears. *Dedication*. And how important that is. We cannot hope to reach the heights of fashion without dedication. They're not called "the heights" by accident. Oh, no. We are like mountain climbers, and, to reach our goal, we need a combination of vision, and planning, and hard, hard work.'

She spread her arms.

'What do our friends across the Channel say?'

Everyone chanted again.

'*Il faut souffrir pour être belle.*'

Bonny nudged Araminta. 'What's that?'

'French,' Araminta said. 'It means: "*You have to suffer to be beautiful.*" It's our Charm School motto.' She laid her hand on Bonny's arm. 'Well,' she said. 'You tell me, now you've heard all that, can you really understand how Pearl can find it even a tiny bit boring?'

'No,' Bonny admitted honestly. 'I wasn't bored. I thought Suki's shopping story was *fascinating*.'

(As fascinating as any other amazing tale, she added privately to herself. Like people putting their heads in lions' jaws, or walking on tightropes over deepest canyons.)

But Araminta just looked thrilled that Bonny agreed with her. 'Oh, I'm so glad! The moment I saw you, I thought, "Here's someone I can tell things, and she'll understand". And I was right!' Ecstatically, she swirled. The white shawl glittered, entrancing Bonny into silence as Araminta twirled towards the door.

'I'll go and borrow Pearl to be our stand-in while I show you what I know about the lights. I'll tell Mrs Opalene that, since there's no sign of Maura yet, we need a little bit of help, just for a while. She won't be pleased. But she's got a marshmallow heart, so we'll get round her somehow.'

Bonny watched, still enchanted, as Araminta tripped lightly up behind the one she called Pearl, and patted her arm gently. As Pearl twisted in her seat to listen, her dark curls caught the light. Then her eyes sparkled to match, and in an instant she was on her feet, begging Mrs Opalene, 'Oh, please! You do say how nice it is always to try to be helpful! Do let me go and be the stand-in for them. Oh, please! Oh, *please!*'

Mrs Opalene looked anxious. 'But, Pearl, dear, we're just getting to the hints on how to make a face pack out of oatmeal. Surely you wouldn't want to miss that.'

Pearl cast around desperately. 'Suki could tell me all about it afterwards, Mrs Opalene. I could even copy out her notes. Or Cindy-Lou's.'

'Oh, very well, then,' Mrs Opalene agreed reluctantly. 'Just for a few moments, since Maura's obviously held up in traffic or something and this new Miss Sparky's having a bit of trouble finding her way around our lovely new equipment.'

Already Pearl was scrambling up onto the stage. Mrs Opalene looked shocked. 'Pearl, dear. Do go round and walk up the steps nicely,' she added hastily, with a shudder. 'I do think that would be a little more *charming*.'

Blushing, Pearl scrambled back down, and tried to walk in hurried fairy footsteps. Suddenly Bonny noticed that no-one in the circle had eyes for anyone but Pearl. Some had little smiles on their faces, and some were merely looking a bit smug. But it was

obvious what most of them were thinking. In Pearl's great rush to get away from Handy Hints, she hadn't been walking as if she were on the brink of dancing. And when she was pleading with Mrs Opalene, she hadn't been talking as if she were about to burst into song. So that was two black marks for Pearl. She was a whole lot less likely to be crowned the Supreme Queen, and walk off with the glistering tiara.

While Araminta was busy settling Pearl into the right position, Bonny looked round the circle of smiles and wondered if they could really be as gloating and creepy as she thought. For if these Charm School girls and Little Miss Pretties couldn't help showing how pleased they were when someone forgot to act like a simpering princess for just two minutes, then what on earth would they be like the day someone in their class at school showed up with braces on her teeth, or a spot on her nose?

It was a nasty thought.

In hurried Araminta. 'Quick!' she said. 'Before Mrs Opalene loses her patience and orders Pearl back in the circle. Watch this!'

She took the swivel chair and spun to face Pearl through the glass wall. 'Look at her standing there. Perfectly normal. Right?'

'Right,' Bonny agreed, moving closer.

'Look,' said Araminta. She flicked a switch, and pointed. Now Pearl was standing on the stage with only a black smudge for a face.

'That's backlight shining from behind,' Araminta explained. 'So all you see is that weird halo of light round her hair, and a glow through her ears.'

Miss Cute Candy was eyeing Bonny up and down.

'Where's all your stuff?'

'I haven't got any.'

'What, none? No make-up? Nothing for your nails? No stuff to fix your hair?'

Poor Bonny's heart was sinking. 'No. None of that.'

'I don't see why you're even here,' said Miss Cute Candy. 'What's the point of showing up if all you're going to be is One Big Nothing?'

Forced to spend a day at Charm School while her mother is on a course, Bonny makes some surprising — and hilarious — discoveries . . .

When one gets dirty, you just pull the next out of the cupboard. You don't have to waste half your life standing in front of the mirror, worrying.' He plucked at the shirt he was wearing and squeaked at Bonny. 'Now tell me the truth! Does this shirt look exactly right? Does the green go with the grey of the trousers?'

'Everything goes with grey,' Bonny said. But he wasn't listening. He was still doing his imitation. 'No, don't spare my feelings! If they're not an absolute match, I swear I'll trail round twenty shops till I find a colour that's *perfect*.'

'Twenty shops is nothing,' scoffed Bonny. 'Suki in there went round forty to find the right choker.'

'Really?' The tea boy peered at Suki through the glass. 'I think I'd just pick the one I liked best in the first shop, then go off fishing.'

'So would my dad,' said Bonny. 'Mum says that's why men's clothes are always the first things you come to in big stores. Because, if you had to drag them any further, they wouldn't go.'

'Too busy,' said the tea boy. 'Better things to

do than trail round shopping every time the fashions change.' He picked up the microphone and pretended to make a news announcement. *'To no-one's astonishment, men's favourite trouser colours will remain the easy-to-match, stain-hiding dark range, and their hems will stay at ankle length for yet another season.'* He grinned at Bonny. 'And, believe me,' he added, 'no-one will even notice.'

'Unless you forget to put them on.'

'Oh, yes.' He snatched up Araminta's shawl. 'Or if they're all spangly, like this.' Swirling it round, he held it flat against his body. 'Toby, the Glittering Man!'

'Very flash,' agreed Bonny, thinking how odd he looked. When Araminta wore the shawl, she'd just looked special – all dressed up and fancy. But Toby immediately looked like a clown, or an actor in a pantomime, or the comedy star of some Christmas Variety Spectacular. Bonny was used to seeing women glitter. (Just look at Mrs Opalene.) But men don't go round glittering unless they're inviting you to share a laugh. No-one takes seriously someone who is twinkling. Bonny realised for the first time why lawyers

and bankers went to work in sober suits, and police officers and traffic wardens wore dark uniforms. It would be hard to pay them nearly so much attention if they were dressed in frothy clothes, with flashing rhinestone earrings. Trousers that twinkle say only, 'Look! Look at me!' Plain skirts and jackets (like Mrs Sullivan's at school) say, 'Now listen carefully. This is important.' Or—

The spell was clearly working overtime, because the next thing Bonny heard Toby say was, 'Hey! You're not listening!'

'No, sorry,' Bonny said. 'I was too busy watching you twinkle.'

'What I was saying,' repeated Toby, draping Araminta's shawl over the chair, 'is that lunch will be ready in five minutes.'

'Goody. I'm starving. I'll be first in the queue.'

'Which queue?' he asked. 'The queue for the smallest heap of beans? Or the thinnest slice of bread? Or the tiniest dab of butter?'

'Don't they even eat at *mealtimes*?'

'Eat!' Toby said. '*Eat*? Oh, you'll see one or two of them pushing the odd shred of lettuce around their plates, and nibbling at stalks of celery. You might even spot one of them

looking longingly at a sliver of grilled fish; or gingerly dipping her spoon into a tiny tub of non-fat, low-calorie yoghurt. But what you and I would call *eating?* No, you won't see any of that.'

'*They* will, though,' Bonny said drily. 'They'll see *me*.'

They didn't simply see. They sat and *stared*. (All except Araminta, who stood as far from Bonny as she could in the long canteen queue, then took a seat at the far end of the table.) None of the rest of them could take their eyes off Bonny's double slice of pizza and her tossed salad.

Bonny took her first mouthfuls, and looked round in hopes of seeing her mother. But, clearly, the victims of Bookkeeping (Advanced) were kept miserably hungry as well as horribly busy. And, anyway, Pearl was tapping her on her sleeve.

'You do realize,' she was saying kindly, 'that that dressing you've put on your salad is mostly oil?'

Bonny gave it some thought. 'I can taste vinegar in it,' she said after a moment. 'And a little bit of garlic.'

'Yes,' chimed in Cindy-Lou. 'But Pearl is right. It's mostly oil.'

Bonny was mystified. 'What's wrong with that? Olive oil tastes nice. And it's good for you.'

'It's a hundred and fifty calories a *tablespoonful*,' said Cristalle firmly, as if that settled the matter. Simply to keep the peace, Bonny shifted her fork across to her pizza.

Suki's mouth dropped open. 'Are you really going to eat that?' she couldn't help asking.

'Yes.' Bonny stared at her. 'That's why I took it.'

Now everyone was chiming in. '*All* of it? *Both slices?*'

'As well as the salad dressing?'

'*Now?*'

'Those croutons look to me as if they're *fried*,' added Cristalle, as if the word meant '*poisonous*'.

Bonny tried to ignore them all. Keeping her head well down, she watched the food on their own plates. Toby was right. All that they seemed to do was shuffle it round and round, making a giant great fuss of it, but never actually putting any of it in their mouths. Bonny watched, fascinated, as Esmeralda made a great show of reaching for a slice of bread, then unwrapping her butter pat. It took her twenty times as long as it would have taken Bonny to peel the shiny foil off the tiny yellow square and fold the foil up neatly. Then Esmeralda picked up her knife and started to mash the butter on her plate.

'What are you doing?'

'Just softening the butter.'

'Why?'

'It spreads better,' said Esmeralda.

And thinner, too. Bonny watched Esmeralda smear the tiniest fraction of butter onto her bread, and make a great display of spreading it around, though there was so little of it, it was practically invisible.

'Aren't you using the rest up?'

'Gosh, no.' Esmeralda looked horrified. 'This is *tons*.'

She still wasn't actually eating it, Bonny noticed. Now she was neatly cutting the slice into quarters. And, after that, each quarter into strips. And then she trimmed each crust

off, one by one. Anyone glancing her way would be left with the impression that she was bent over her plate tucking in happily. But she still hadn't eaten anything.

Bonny leaned over the table and tapped her fork beside Esmeralda's plate. In a nannyish voice, she said to her, 'Stop playing with your food, dear!'

Esmeralda looked up, startled. 'What do you mean?'

'Just what I say,' said Bonny, still in her nanny voice. 'Stop messing, and eat it.'

'I *am* eating,' said Esmeralda.

'No, you're not,' Bonny said, going back to her normal voice to explain what she meant. 'What you're doing is shunting and mashing and smearing and slicing. But you're not actually *eating* anything. So, apart from the fact that you're doing it so daintily, you're just messing with your food like a giant great baby.'

Esmeralda went scarlet. 'I am not! I *am* eating. I have eaten *tons*.'

'*What?* Tell us *what*.'

'I ate most of the lettuce. And the fishcake. And the beans.'

'You didn't eat the fishcake,' Suki said. 'You hid it under the lettuce. With the beans.'

Bonny reached over and lifted Esmeralda's lettuce with her fork. Esmeralda blushed as the evidence was displayed around the table. But several of the others were blushing too. Bonny turned to her right and lifted Amethyst's largest lettuce leaf with the fork. Out peeped two fish fingers and some mushrooms. She turned to her left, and Serena snatched her plate away.

'It's none of your business!'

'You have to eat,' said Bonny. 'If you don't eat, your brain doesn't work properly, and you get all tearful and crabby.'

There was a whisper further up the table, and everyone giggled.

'What was that?' asked Bonny.

'Nothing,' said Sarajane. 'Angelica just made a little joke, that's all.'

'What did you say?' Bonny asked Angelica.

'Nothing,' said Angelica.

'No, go on,' insisted Bonny. 'Share the joke.'

'I've forgotten,' said Angelica.

'I haven't,' said Serena, getting her own back on Angelica for being so spiteful about the smell of her perfume. She leaned towards Bonny. 'When you said that people who don't eat get all tearful and crabby, Angelica said,

"Better than getting all fat like her".'

'All fat like who?'

Everyone was silent. Even Araminta was watching now. And Angelica looked very embarrassed.

Bonny looked down at herself. 'Do you mean *me*?'

Still no-one spoke. Bonny pushed back her chair and looked at herself. She was the exact same shape she'd been when she left home that morning. She wasn't built from matchsticks, it was true. Her legs weren't thin glass rods. You couldn't have spread your hands round her waist and touched your own fingers.

But she wasn't fat.

She was perfectly normal.

Pushing her chair back even further, Bonny looked round the table.

'You should stop worrying about how much you have on your bodies,' she told them. 'And start worrying about how little you have in your heads. No wonder the tea boy calls you all Twinks.'

'*Twinks*?'

'Toby?'

They were outraged.

'He does *not.*'

'Don't listen to her. She's just saying mean things to upset us.'

Bonny pointed a finger at Lulu, who was the last to speak. 'Oh, no, I'm not! Toby agrees with me. He thinks you're all silly and vain. And you *are*,' she added fiercely. 'You spend your whole lives trailing round shops, and parked on your bums trying to look prettier than the person beside you, and strolling round being spiteful to one another. So why should anyone think you have more than half a brain between you?'

Now Cristalle was shaking her finger back at Bonny. 'You're wrong!' she snapped. 'Quite wrong! Toby actually thinks that we're something rather special. That's why he spends as much time as he can watching us through the glass window.'

'Oh no, it's not,' said Bonny. 'He watches you because he can't get over how daffy you are.'

'How wrong can you get, Miss Clever Sparky? I tell you, Toby *likes* us.' Cristalle gave an arch look across the table to Sarajane. 'Especially *one* of us,' she added meaningfully. 'There does happen to be one

♥111♥

of us he *really* likes ...'

At this, everyone turned to look at Sarajane, who blushed bright pink. But Bonny barely noticed. '*You're* the ones who've got it wrong,' she was too busy insisting. 'He doesn't *like* you all. You just *amuse* him.'

Sarajane's blush turned fiery red, and Esmeralda said loudly to no-one in particular, 'Talk about other people being spiteful! She should try listening to *herself.*'

There was another giggle and more whispering at the other end of the table. This time Bonny was quicker swinging round, and out of the corner of her eye, she saw Araminta dart a look at her, then hastily shut her mouth and wipe an amused smile off her face.

Bonny was astonished at how upset she felt – as if a real, true friend had turned against her. She felt tears gathering and her voice was shaky. 'I suppose *you're* being nasty about me now.'

Araminta looked horribly guilty. But it was Lulu at her side who broke the awkward silence. Putting on that sugared poison voice Bonny had heard so often that morning as people said their horrid things, she explained very kindly to Bonny: 'Oh, no. Minty was try-

ing to be *nice*. You see, she was explaining to us all why you can't help being so rude and disagreeable.'

Minty! They all had one another as friends, and she had none! Miserable as she could be, Bonny said crossly, 'Oh, really? Why is that, then?'

As she spoke, she tried looking Araminta straight in the eye, but Araminta hastily stared down at the table. 'It doesn't matter,' she mumbled very uncomfortably. 'I've quite forgotten what I said.'

Once again, Miss Pass-on-the-Spite Serena pitched in to help someone who'd lost her memory. She leaned over to Bonny.

'*I* haven't, though. Minty was just explaining that you were simply jealous.'

'Jealous?' Now it was Bonny's turn to be outraged. '*Jealous?* Of all you noodle-brained *ninnies*? Of all you flopsy-mopsy *beanbrains*? Oh, I don't think so!' Then, suddenly remembering you couldn't trust what any of them said when they were causing trouble, she leaned across the table and said to Araminta, 'Is that *true*?'

Araminta flushed even redder than Sarajane had earlier. 'Is what true?'

'What she just said. That you told them I was jealous.'

Araminta didn't answer. Bonny rose to her feet. 'Is it?' she demanded again. 'Is it true? Is that what you said?'

Again, Araminta took refuge in mumbling. 'I've quite forgotten. I can't remember what I said at all.'

'You can't remember?' Bonny leaned over the table. 'Well, I did warn you, if you don't eat, your brain stops working properly.' She picked up her plate. 'What you need, Araminta, is a proper meal, and I've got one here for you!'

All Bonny's fury and upset boiled up in her. And boiled over. And before Araminta could even twist her head aside, Bonny had slapped the lukewarm plate of pizza in her face, and ground it round.

Everyone squealed, and Araminta clawed at the dripping mess of cheese and tomato and onion. Her huge shocked saucer eyes peered out in horror, like two rounds of pepperoni.

'There!' Bonny snapped. 'Feeling any better?'

And off she stomped, in a foul temper, out of the canteen and up the back stairs, all alone, back to Charm School.

CHAPTER FOUR

'Y ou have to hand it to Mrs Opalene,'
Toby remarked on his next visit. 'You
start a riot, and before she's even finished ticking you off properly, she's somehow
managed to turn it into a class about taking
off make-up.'

And so she had. As soon as it became clear
Bonny was stubbornly going to stick to her
story of tripping as she so kindly cleared
away Araminta's unfinished meal, Mrs
Opalene had simply given her one last, help-
less, reproachful look, then turned to poor
dripping Araminta.

Holding her at arm's length, she said, with as much enthusiasm as she could muster:

'Marvellous! The perfect opportunity to try out some cleansers! Thank you, dear Araminta, for giving us a chance to do some real *testing*.'

Bonny felt terrible. She'd been so rude about poor Mrs Opalene. Yet here she was, valiantly making the best of things, scraping the worst of the pizza off with little balls of cotton wool till, gradually, Araminta's tearful face emerged through the tomato-stained cheese streaks.

'There! Splendid! Now we'll divide your face into four separate sections, and try a different cleanser on each, to see which comes out best.' She looked around. 'Now who would like to be first to show us their gentle cleansing technique?'

Araminta's sobs quietened as Pearl stepped forward eagerly. 'Oh, please! Can I have a go with that green glop?'

Mrs Opalene threw up her hands. 'That green glop! That green glop!' Lifting the tiny plastic tub of cream at which Pearl had been pointing, she rebuked her errant pupil. 'Pearl, dear, this is Glow Girl's phytolyastil

♥117♥

V.I.A. Complex tissue peptide VHJ with hygragscopic elements and natural ceramides, and a syntropic blend of unique Derma Bio Tropocollagen. You may not simply call it "glop".'

'Sorry,' said Pearl, chastened.

Toby nudged Bonny. 'Looks like glop to me.'

'And me.'

'Stroke it on *gently*, dear,' Mrs Opalene was telling Pearl. 'Don't *scrape* away at Araminta's precious face. And, as with all our little skin helpers, dears, what must we always remember?'

She waved her hands like a conductor as all of them chorused dutifully.

'*Smeary is dreary*, Mrs Opalene.'

'Smeary is dreary!' Bonny flipped off the sound. 'Phytolyastil!' she muttered scornfully. 'Tissue peptides! It's just pretend science, so they can charge the earth for every teaspoon. But Pearl's quite right. All it is really is glop.

And if everyone suddenly stopped feeling halfway to ugly, all those glop factories would close overnight.'

'Someone would lose an awful lot of money if that happened.'

'But everyone else would keep a lot more.'

'The factory owners ought to pay Mrs Opalene to run this Charm School,' Toby said. 'In come these perfectly normal girls, and only one of them can end up winning the glistering tiara. So all the rest go home feeling like rubbish, and buy more glop.'

'And clothes.'

'And jewellery.'

'And shoes.'

'And perfume.'

'And nail stuff.'

'And hair stuff.'

'And beauty books and magazines.' She stared at Toby, horrified. 'That's what it's all for, really, isn't it? To make them buy more stuff. On and on and on. And, if they're not buying fast enough, you simply tell them that swimsuits look different this year.'

'Or handbags have to be made out of raffia.'

'Or pink is *yesterday*'s colour.'

'It's like having an exam every day. And

every now and then you get to have a big exam, like this. One of them gets to come top and be the Supreme Queen.'

'And all the rest go home feeling ugly, and think they ought to try harder. So they waste even more of their time shopping, and even more of their money on stuff to try to look nicer.'

'And they can't even cheer themselves up by having two slices of pizza. They have to go round half-starved in case they put on a quarter of an ounce.'

'And think their legs have turned into pillars in a multi-storey car park.' She turned to Toby. 'It's very clever, really, isn't it? *Too* clever ...'

Toby eyed her curiously. 'What do you mean?'

'Just what I say. It's *too* clever. Hard to believe it's all a sort of accident.'

'You don't think someone *planned* it?'

'Wouldn't you?'

'Who? Some evil band of fat glop factory owners, sailing off on luxury holidays with all the loot they've made?'

'Laughing up their sleeves at all the silly people they've fooled into buying yet another set of clothes.'

'Because sleeves are much puffier this year.'

'Or skirts are much straighter.' She narrowed her eyes suspiciously. 'You know, I wouldn't be at all surprised if they owned all the glossy magazines as well. Wouldn't that be the cleverest thing? And wouldn't it be a cheek? First, you rip everyone off by selling them forty pages of "fashion news". And then you sit back and watch them trailing round the shops like sheep, ripping themselves off by buying stuff they'd never have thought of, without you.'

'No wonder they're laughing.'

Bonny turned to stare through the glass. 'Do you suppose that Mrs Opalene is in on it?'

'Mrs Opalene? In the pay of the glop men? Do you really think so?'

'I don't know.'

Together they watched Mrs Opalene. As usual, she was all excited about something. This time it appeared to be yet another of the pretty tubes and pots and bottles spread on the table top at her side.

Bonny flicked up the sound.

'... with lanoline filtrate and a specially selected cationic derivative ...'

Bonny flicked the sound down again.

'I don't know,' Toby said dubiously. 'She's never sounded like a fake to me. And she has such an honest face. I honestly think she *believes* it.'

'Sincerely? *All* of it?'

Now it was Toby's turn to flick up the sound.

'... with that super protein conditioning that does so much to adjust the P.H. balance and improve the *texture* of ...'

He flicked it down.

'She wouldn't have to be one of the gang,' he said. 'In fact, it probably works better for them if she truly believes everything she says.'

'Then she can't turn on them. Or spill the beans.'

'She'll just go round her whole life, spreading the word like a preacher.'

'*Smeary is dreary. You have to suffer to be beautiful.* Yes.' Bonny swivelled on the chair. 'It's about as clever a plan as you can get. You set it off with a few fancy photographs, and then sit back and watch people like Mrs Opalene rush in and keep it going.'

'Like unpaid police officers herding every-

one along in the right direction.'

'*Walk as if you were dancing!*' Bonny mimicked bitterly. '*Smile nicely. Twirl neatly. Keep your knees together.* And when she's not around, there's all those little beauty helpers of hers to keep it going.' Again, she was mimicking. '*You're not going to eat* both *those slices of pizza, are you? Do you realize it's* fried? *You don't look as if you fell to earth from Planet Fashion.*'

'They can be a whole lot worse than that,' said Toby. 'At least the police have rest days. This lot never stop going on at one another, keeping themselves up to scratch.' He flicked on the microphones in the corners of the room, where Mrs Opalene's girls were scattering to get themselves ready for the Curls and Purls Show.

Both of them listened.

'I think you should get your hair highlighted again,' Serena was telling Cindy-Lou. 'It's beginning to look just that tiny bit mousy.'

'Perhaps the pink frock suits your colouring better,' Amethyst was suggesting to Angelica.

'Are those split ends in your hair?' Sarajane was asking Esmeralda. 'Maybe it's time for a trim.'

'Your hem's just the tiniest bit uneven,' Lulu was warning Suki. 'Though it hardly shows at all from the front.'

Bonny shook her head. 'I don't know how they can stand it. It's like listening to dripping taps.'

They eavesdropped some more.

'Fat people should never, *ever* tuck in their blouses,' Cristalle was pontificating firmly. 'It makes them look awful. Just *awful*.'

'You should always smile in a mirror to check your teeth after eating spinach,' Pearl was telling Araminta.

'You should never wear aubergine eye

shadow with a pink top,' Cindy-Lou was explaining to Cooki. 'The colours simply *shriek* at one another.'

'Always rest your weight on your back leg, and point the other towards the camera,' Pearl was informing Sarajane.

'So many *rules*,' Toby said wonderingly. '"You must *always* ...", "You should *never* ...".'

'The magazines are full of rules,' Bonny told him. 'Well, not even rules, really. *Orders.* Don't wear this with that! Rub this in your face before you paint that on! Walk like this! Sit like that!'

'It was like that in my nursery school,' Toby remembered. 'Hang up your coat nicely! Put your wellies in the corner! Wash your hands before snack-time!'

'But you were *four.*'

'If any magazine I bought kept giving me orders,' Toby said, 'I'd chuck it in the nearest bin.'

'But they just try a bit harder.'

They watched Serena struggling into her outfit.

'They don't even buy clothes that fit them,' Toby observed ruefully. 'They force their bodies into fitting the clothes.' He pointed

through the glass. 'Look at her face. She's astonished that she's managed to fasten that waistband.'

'No, she's not,' Bonny corrected him. 'She's just striking a pose. Esmeralda's probably just told her "amazed" is her best look and makes her eyes look big and round.'

Toby turned away in disgust, but Bonny couldn't help carrying on watching.

'They're like caged birds,' she said. 'The door's wide open, but instead of flying off, they spend their whole time making pretty Milly the Model poses on their perches, and fluffing up their feathers.'

'Mrs Opalene's been running this Charm School for years,' Toby told Bonny. 'Some of them must have broken out and got a life. Why haven't this lot followed?'

'Because they don't see why the others left. When someone decides, "This is a waste of time," and stomps off home to do something more interesting, all of them think, "Oh, she's just a bad loser. She's leaving because she knows she'll never win."'

'Perhaps they wouldn't be quite so happy to stay in their cages if you told them Mrs Opalene was part of a horrible plot to take

their money and use up their lives.'

'They'd never believe me,' said Bonny. 'They all think she's wonderful – so kind and encouraging. Look how she didn't even order me out after the fuss with the pizza, in case there'd be no lights or music for their precious show.' Bonny pointed at radiant, shawl-swirling Araminta. 'Besides,' she added forlornly, '*she's* already told them all that I'm just jealous.'

Again it came, that pang of something precious, lost for ever. She turned to Toby for comfort. But, he, too, was staring wistfully out through the glass.

'You'd think that, if you'd already managed to win that stupid glistering tiara of theirs at least once, you'd be able to stop bothering. But you take that lovely, raven-haired Sarajane. She was Miss Sweet Caroline *ages* ago. But still she seems to do nothing at all except worry about what she looks like.'

He looked so mournful that Bonny couldn't help remembering Cristalle's arch look at lunch, and Sarajane's blush. To try and cheer him she put her irritation with the girls aside and stuck up for Sarajane. 'She probably tries

to think about other things. But then I expect she goes out and sees a hundred posters of pretty girls with slim long legs. Or she switches on the television and sees advertisements of girls with perfect hair. Or she goes to the cinema and sees dozens of actresses with beautiful faces.'

He made an impatient gesture. 'Someone should tell her the photographs are all touched up. And models go round practically *chained* to their hairdressers. And most of the adverts for tights and swimsuits have the models' legs stretched on computer, to look longer and slimmer.'

Bonny shrugged. 'I expect they've been told all that already. But just so long as somewhere in the world there's one perfect person—'

'One beautiful, hair-flicking Amethyst ...'

'—they'll all just keep on trying.' Bonny sighed. 'But you are right. Somebody ought to try and rescue them.'

'Not me,' Toby said hastily. 'I have to get back to the tea room before someone comes looking for me. And you should be getting on with sorting things out for their silly Curls and Purls show.'

'I suppose it's better than just sitting in here watching them. That's really sad.'

'Don't feel too sorry for them. That's what they like most, being looked at.' He pulled the door open. 'Feel sorry for their poor friends. Listening to people fussing about clothes and hair and how much weight they've put on is even more boring than being dragged around the shops watching someone look for clothes they don't need.'

Bonny grinned mischievously. 'Maybe some girls go to all this trouble to look nice for *you* ...'

He waggled a finger at her. 'Don't kid yourself. I couldn't give a bean. No, they're doing it to impress one another, and make a heap more money for the glop men.'

The glop men ... As Toby hurried off, Bonny turned back to the glass. Could it be some great conspiracy? Like Toby, Bonny found it hard to believe that Mrs Opalene's beaming, enthusiastic face masked some vile plan to steal people's money by making them feel awful. After all, boys and men wasted time and money too. Look at the hours and hours her father spent slumped on the sofa watching eleven men – or was it twelve? – kicking

some stupid ball up and down the pitch, then listening to even bigger idiots drivelling on about how they must be "over the moon", or "totally gutted". At least the girls could sing and dance, and knew how to wear their clothes properly. The boy next door spent all his money on new football stuff, and his team changed it time and again. He didn't get to decide when to stop wearing it. The team manager decided for him. That was fashion too.

Her head was spinning. She was almost glad when bossy Cristalle poked her great puffy-haired head around the door and said to her officiously, 'Nearly time to start! Pass me that box, please.'

Bonny looked behind her. There on the shelf was a box labelled 'Number discs'. She handed it over. Cristalle disappeared, and Bonny turned up the microphones to hear what was happening.

In the far corner, Mrs Opalene was putting the final touches to Lulu's cowboy-sweetheart costume. Lulu was pouting at herself in the mirror.

'Look at me! I look *terrible*.'

'I think you look very nice, dear.'

'No, I don't! I've got bags under my eyes,

and skin so dry it's almost cracking.'

Mrs Opalene tilted Lulu's pretty gingham mob hat a tiny bit to the side. 'Does that look better?' She leaned over to inspect the pouting face in the mirror. 'Have you been going round without a sun hat, dear? I hope you haven't been forgetting the names of your dreaded Skin Enemies.'

'No, Mrs Opalene.'

'So you can tell me who they are?'

Lulu's answer came promptly enough. 'Sun. And Misery.'

'That's right, dear. And who are your precious Skin Helpers?'

'Sleep,' Lulu said dutifully. 'And Water. Lots of water.' Her face fell. 'I've forgotten the third one.'

Mrs Opalene looked pained.

'Oh, no, I haven't!' cried Lulu. 'It's Fresh Air!'

'Splendid!' declared Mrs Opalene. 'With plenty of sleep and water and fresh air, our skin can't go wrong!'

Ignoring Lulu's bad-tempered muttering – 'Well, *mine* has!' – Mrs Opalene sailed off to help Esmeralda with her ruffles. Bonny shook her head, mystified. Sleep. Water.

Fresh Air. All not just cheap, but *free*. How could Mrs Opalene be part of some fiendish plot to take people's money? Surely if that were true, then she'd be busy trying to persuade poor Lulu that what she needed was a costly pot of Glamour-Puss face cream, or an expensive tube of Skin-So-Soft. And now Bonny thought about it, even when Mrs Opalene had been going on earlier about face packs and elbow bleachers and stuff like that, she'd always saved her real enthusiasm for using up things like squeezed lemon halves, and old breakfast oatmeal.

No money in those. Anyone trying to help the glop men get rich quick would definitely have had the sense to say that only Rich-Girl-Bio-Face-Soothe-With-Added-Lano-Smarm-And-Derma-Tested-Gloss-Glaze (at twenty pounds a tub) would do the trick on Lulu's face.

And Mrs Opalene hadn't.

In fact, she'd said as many sensible as silly things. Keep off the fried foods. Eat fresh fruit and vegetables. Drink plain old water, not those sugary fizzy drinks. It might have been Bonny's mother talking. Toby was right. She must believe it all. The only problem was

that she took it all so seriously. And so did they. It had become the only thing that mattered. It was the most important thing in their lives. Somehow, with all this fussing, they had forgotten how very rich and big and deep living could be. When Bonny thought about it, she realized that, all that morning, she'd never once heard any one of them turn to another and say, 'I missed you at swim club' (Wouldn't that muss up their hair!) or 'Are you coming camping this weekend?' (What scruffs they'd end up looking!) or even 'Meet you in the library on Saturday morning?' (Oh, no. They'd miss a whole four hours down the shops!)

No, Bonny thought glumly, watching them twirling and spinning and practising their prettiest faces. They were doomed. They had become like all those prissy milksops in the poems, walking in beauty but not going anywhere.

It was her job to save them, that was obvious.

But *how*? She couldn't go and talk to them because she was too busy with the sound and the lighting. And even those who weren't warming up were still frantically putting the last special touches to their make-up or their

hair or their fancy costumes. They hadn't time to listen. And bossy Cristalle was already striding around with the box that she'd taken from Bonny's room.

'Time to choose places!'

One by one, each of them shut her eyes (carefully, so as not to smudge her make-up), whispered her own particular lucky chant, and picked out a coloured disc stamped with a number.

'Eight!' Cooki chortled. 'It's my lucky number!'

Lulu inspected her own disc. 'Five.' She groaned. 'Right in the middle. Who's going to remember anything you do if you're right in the middle?'

'One!' Serena's eyes shone with delight, though she said in pretend horror, 'Oh, it's *awful* going first. It's just horrible! Horrible!'

Cindy-Lou picked her number. 'Goody! I'm last! Everyone remembers the last one.'

One by one, each of them peeled the paper backing off their disc, and stuck the number on their music tape before bringing it to Bonny. They hadn't forgotten the incident with the pizza, she could tell. But no-one wanted to

get on the wrong side of her before the show, so they were all smiles and sweet voices.

'You will remember how I want my spotlight, won't you?'

'If I sing too softly, please turn down the backing tape.'

'My floodlights must stay on for the whole dance, you know.'

'Don't forget that my drum rolls get louder and louder.'

Bonny took notes, and put the tapes in order carefully. After all, if she was going to try and save them, it would be a whole lot easier if they liked and trusted her, and all that squabbling at the lunch table hadn't made the best start in that. So she was as friendly as she could be, nodding and smiling as they trooped in, and reassuring them

when, terribly nervous, they explained what they wanted again, over and over.

And all the time Bonny was secretly hoping that Araminta would come in again, just to check about her lights and her snowflakes. This time, Bonny would get things right. First she would say how sorry she was the two of them had ended up quarrelling so horribly earlier. Then she'd apologize again, about the pizza. After that, she'd throw herself on Araminta's mercy, and beg her help in telling everyone how they were being used, and how they could be so much happier if they had other things to think about than just being pretty. Bonny worked it out in her mind. Araminta would sidle in, looking a little bit pouty and nervous. But once she was absolutely sure Bonny meant what she said, she'd listen carefully. When Bonny explained about the glop men, Araminta would look shocked, and say, 'Oh, let me help. We must explain to everyone. And now we're friends again, please call me Minty.'

So it was almost a surprise when Araminta pushed open the door and stood there, not halfway ready to be friends again, but scowling horribly.

Bonny stepped forward. 'I'm glad you've come. I was just going out to find you, to say I'm sorry.'

Araminta didn't smile.

'About the pizza? Or about being so mean to me earlier?'

Bonny was irritated, but she kept her temper.

'Mostly the pizza. After all, you were mean to me, too.'

'Not nearly as mean as you were.'

'Oh, please don't let's argue,' Bonny said. 'Shoving a pizza in someone's face may be worse than telling everyone that someone's jealous. But I said sorry first, and that's harder than anything.'

Araminta was still making a grumpy I'm-not-convinced face. The meeting really wasn't going as Bonny expected. But she pressed on, because it was important.

'But we have to be friends again, because I really need your help.'

'My help? Why?'

She looked so suspicious that Bonny knew it wouldn't work. Araminta wasn't going to listen. And, if she did, she wouldn't be convinced. And, if she were, she wouldn't help.

It was quite hopeless.

Or was it? In a flash, the idea came.

'Oh,' Bonny said innocently. 'I just had a little plan.'

'A little plan?'

'To please Mrs Opalene, so she'll forgive me for behaving so badly.'

'Please Mrs Opalene…?' Araminta's eyes lit up, as Bonny knew they would. Then she made a face, and said contemptuously, 'Now how would someone like you be able to please Mrs Opalene? It's impossible. She only has to look at you now, to get nervous. There's nothing you could do that would please her, except not cause any more trouble.'

'There is,' said Bonny. 'And I'm going to do it.'

Again, the glint shone in Araminta's eyes. 'What?'

'I wouldn't tell anyone else,' said Bonny. 'But I'll tell you. I'm going to brighten up the Curls and Purls Show.'

'Brighten it up?' Araminta looked doubtful. 'Why should—?'

'Listen,' interrupted Bonny. 'How many Curls and Purls shows have you been in, Araminta?'

'This is my seventh,' Araminta said.

♥138♥

'And how many do you think Mrs Opalene has judged?'

Araminta rolled her eyes upwards as she did the counting. 'Well, she's been running them since my half-sister went to Hooper Road School, and now she's getting on for twenty-two, and there are three a year, and so—' Araminta's eyes widened. 'She must have watched nearly fifty!'

'Exactly!' said Bonny. 'Fifty Curls and Purls shows. She must have seen every dance and heard every song a dozen times. I think she'd be delighted if someone fixed up something different. I bet she'd love a big surprise.'

Araminta was weakening, Bonny could tell. The Charm School girls would all do anything to please Mrs Opalene (especially on the day she chose the winner of the glistering tiara!). Bonny felt a bit bad about being so sneaky with someone who had come so close to being her friend, and whom she'd already upset by covering in pizza. But it was all in a good cause. The girls really should be saved from wasting any more of their lives.

So, leaning closer, Bonny whispered in Araminta's ear.

'Don't you think Mrs Opalene would be thrilled with someone who arranged a nice surprise for her? Something really *different*? Just for once? Don't you think she might even want to give them extra points?'

Araminta drew breath sharply. 'Extra points?'

'Not for me, obviously,' Bonny said casually. 'Because I'm not in the competition.'

'I am, though,' Araminta said, thinking fast.

'Oh, yes,' said Bonny. 'You are.' She shrugged so innocently. 'I suppose you might end up getting the extra points she would have given me, as well. Why, you might end up getting so many you walk off with the glistering tiara!'

She peeped slyly at Araminta, whose eyes were glinting with desire.

'The glistering tiara! Supreme Queen! Me! Oh, yes!' She spread her arms as if she were catching golden coins falling from heaven. 'Oh, yes! The glistering tiara! *Me!*'

Breaking off suddenly, she turned to Bonny. 'But how do I know I can trust you? You've never seemed to bother about Mrs Opalene having nice surprises before. Quite

the opposite! You've given her several nasty ones. And me, too. So how do I know you're not just trying to get me into trouble? How do I know you don't want to win a crown of your own – the Spiteful Miss Sparky crown?'

Turning on Araminta that same, deeply reproachful, look that Mrs Opalene had given her earlier, Bonny put her hand on her heart and said in all honesty, 'I swear to you, Araminta. I'm doing this for the very, very best of reasons.'

Had she missed something? Did Mrs Opalene dish out marshmallow hearts along with the handy hints every Saturday morning? For suddenly Araminta was smiling happily from ear to ear. Reaching out to take Bonny's hands, she spun her round and round, just like before.

'Yes!' she said excitedly. 'Let's do it! Let's do it together! It'll be enormous fun. And we'll give darling, *darling* Mrs Opalene such a surprise!'

CHAPTER FIVE

Serena was first. Crossing her fingers for luck, she tripped up the steps onto the stage dressed in a frilly white Bo-Peep frock and carrying a crook garlanded with ribbons. Bonny wound the big handle labelled BACKDROP 1, and down behind Serena unfurled a painted farmyard scene, with crooked walls, and horses peering over stable doors. Serena wheeled a cardboard wishing well onto the stage. It had a bucket dangling from its winding bar and painted weeds growing up its side.

Amethyst curled in a neat silver ball, and everyone waited. Out swelled the music. As its busy first bars gave way, within moments, to a more sleepy, going-to-bed sort of melody, the silver ball that was Amethyst gradually uncoiled a little, and the glittering wand waved gracefully in the air. Then she rose to her feet and looked around, making grand gestures of surprise and delight, as if she'd never seen an evening before.

And she'd certainly not seen one like this. It started well enough, with Bonny focusing exactly the right tree shadow shapes onto the stage, and turning the evening through the right shades of darkening blue while switching the stars up more brightly. Amethyst flitted round, flicking her hair prettily and pretending to pat each of the soppy, sloe-eyed creatures that were painted on the backdrop with her starry wand of evening.

'Aaaah!' everyone cooed dutifully when she tapped the baby deer sternly on its head.

'Ooooh!' everyone chorused politely when she shook her finger crossly at the chipmunks.

Amethyst swirled around, pretending to look for the squirrel.

And then she screamed. For from the branch over her head dangled the shadow of a massive spider. Amethyst skidded to an ungainly halt. In the control room, Bonny was jiggling the spider silhouette furiously in front of the lantern, and, on the stage, the spider shadow leaped obediently to the attack.

Amethyst screamed again. She'd secretly wanted something different. But this was horrible. Horrible! The whole stage darkened and the shadows loomed. Out went the stars, as if a cloud had swirled in front of them. Swampy green lights flickered eerily, and strange mists rose. In a frenzy of switch-flicking from Bonny, the baby deer ended up howling like a wolverine, the squirrel snarled, and when a demented chattering began to pour out of one of the loudspeakers behind the backdrop, Araminta suddenly had the bright idea of wheeling it behind the bit with the painted chipmunks, as if they'd suddenly come to life, and flown into a fury.

It was quite terrifying. From side to side ran Amethyst, desperate to find a way off the stage. She wasn't fleeing very elegantly, for all her hours of practice. Each time she

thought she'd found a safe way to go, a shadow shaped like broken fingers seemed to snatch at her, or shadows of branches underfoot snaked out as if to trip her.

Her enthralled audience shouted.

'Try that way, Amethyst!'

'No! It's not safe! Try the other side!'

'Amethyst! Watch out!'

'Look behind you!'

Round and round Amethyst ran, in ever more desperate circles. From behind the backcloth came a werewolf's cry. And then another, sounding even closer.

Amethyst tore at her hair in fright. Sweat glistened on her face, melting her perfect make-up. Her lovely features twisted in terror and in the end she did the only thing that she could think of, and hurled herself back in a silver ball on the floor, covering her eyes with her fingers.

And that's when Bonny switched on the sounds of tiny, scurrying feet. Spreading her fingers slightly, Amethyst saw the little furry balls of shadow flitting across the stage.

'Oh, not rats! No!'

Amethyst jumped to her feet and started beating at them with her glittering wand. As the music came to an end and Bonny regretfully turned up the light to flood the stage with rosy dawn, Amethyst was to be seen clutching her torn skirts around her, still try-

ing to beat to death a dozen skittering rats that were just shadows.

And how the audience clapped.

'Amethyst! Why didn't you tell us you could *act*?'

'My heart's still thumping, Amethyst. You ought to be in horror films! You're brilliant!'

'Do the scream again. Just one more time. It was so *bloodcurdling*.'

'I really thought that was a spider. And the rats fooled me too.'

'The rats fooled *everyone*. Did they fool you, Mrs Opalene?'

Mrs Opalene blinked hastily. It wouldn't do at all to admit that, ever since the spider, she'd had her eyes tightly closed. Not that it had helped much. She had still heard the werewolf's cry, the wolverine's snarl, and the terrified squeals from everyone around her.

Better say something, or they'd force her into watching it again, so she could mark it properly.

'Gratifyingly macabre, dear.'

Amethyst smiled bravely. She didn't know what gratifying meant. Or macabre, either. But now the lights were on again, she could at least get off the stage without falling over

from fright. It hadn't been fun. It had been *terrifying*. But they were all talking about it so excitedly, and patting her on the back as she went shakily back to her seat. Only a minute ago, she could have cheerfully strangled that new Miss Sparky. Miss Electric Shock, more like! But now that her heart had stopped thumping, she could admit to herself that this *Dance of the Evening Star* must have been a whole lot more thrilling to watch than the usual old waking and fluttering and fleeing.

'Next!' called Mrs Opalene faintly.

Up on the stage walked Sarajane. But as Bonny reached for music tape number 4, she saw a shadow fall on the desk in front of her.

Hastily, she swung around.

'Toby!'

He nodded through the glass towards the stage. 'Brilliant!' he told her. 'Stunning! A real spectacular! It's quite amazing how much you've picked up in one short day.'

'Araminta's been helping. It turns out she knows a whole lot more than she ever realized. She's a real star at—'

He wasn't listening. He was looking worried.

'But you must promise me you won't make a fool of Sarajane.'

Bonny couldn't help staring. 'Oh, come on,' she managed to get out at last. 'If it's all right for the others, then it's all right for her. Sarajane is no different.'

'She is to me,' Toby said stubbornly. He blushed. 'I know that she can be as silly as all the others. But still I don't want her ending up head down in a well with her bloomers showing, or singing in her vest and knickers, or running round screaming.'

'Nothing wrong with that,' Bonny said, equally stubbornly. 'They're all enjoying it. You can tell.'

'It doesn't matter if she *does* it,' Toby said. 'It just matters that she gets to *choose*. And you haven't asked her.'

Bonny was silent. It was no more than the

truth. But they were halfway through the show now. She wasn't going to stop for anyone.

Bonny turned back to the controls. 'Sorry, Toby,' she said firmly. 'But I'm afraid Araminta and I are running this show.'

She felt a finger in the small of her back. 'Well, I'm afraid I'm warning you and your very good friend Araminta. Don't mess with Sarajane's song, or you'll regret it.'

Bonny made a face. So Cristalle was right. Toby was soft on Sarajane. But that was no reason for the two of them to change their plans. Araminta had already filled the bucket with water, and what could Toby do to them anyway? The day was very nearly over. How could a tea boy cause trouble for them? It was an empty threat. Of course he couldn't.

And then it struck her. Yes, he could. He could rush down and tell the lady on the desk what she and Araminta were doing, and she could hurry off to fetch Mum out of Bookkeeping (Advanced), and ...

Fetch Mum out of her class? Oh, that would be *awful*. It was so very near the end of the day that she might be in the middle of the test that would give her the certificate she needed so

badly. Why, she might be on the very last question. To be so close, and have to lay down your pen and rush up to the third floor because of your troublesome daughter! What a way to start your new life in a brand new place.

'All right,' said Bonny sourly. 'You win.' But then suddenly, ringing in her ears again as if she'd somehow pressed the 'echo' switch, she heard the little phrase he'd used to warn her so sternly: 'you and your very good friend Araminta'.

And suddenly she didn't mind. Let Sarajane get on and do her bit in the Curls and Purls Show as soppily as she'd planned. If it mattered so much to Toby (and it obviously did), she'd just sit back and watch – with her good friend Araminta!

'All right,' she said again, a whole lot more cheerfully. 'We won't do anything to Sarajane. And that's a promise.'

★ ☀ ♥ ☆

CHAPTER SIX

Bonny slid in the music tape, and
dropped into the revolving lantern the
sheet that threw images of glittering
rain. While Sarajane stood waiting for the
excited chatter of the audience to die away,
Bonny signalled frantically at Araminta to
move to the nearest loudspeaker, then whispered. 'Don't throw the water!'

'Why not?' hissed back Araminta. 'It'll be
brilliant. Everyone will love it.'

Already Sarajane was stepping forward.

'I can't explain,' Bonny whispered hastily.

'There isn't time. But just don't throw it. Don't do *anything*. Promise?'

Araminta shrugged, disappointed. But, like a good friend, she answered trustingly, 'Well, if you say so.'

Sarajane was explaining now. 'This is a lovely little song and dance called *Pretty Miss Raindrop*. It starts with a great peal of thunder so you mustn't be startled. And then I fall to earth in a glittering shower. There aren't many words in the song.' She stopped, embarrassed. 'Well, actually, the only words in it are *'Drip, drip, drip'*. But I do sing them over and over.'

More of a threat than a promise, Bonny thought privately. But she obediently pressed PLAY when Sarajane gave the signal. There was a moment's silence. Then, from the speakers, flowed the plaintive sound of violins.

Bonny waited for the thunderpeal. (Sarajane had told her three times over that this was the cue to switch on the glittering shower.) But nothing like a peal of thunder came, only the music rising and falling like souls lost in grief. Bonny peeked through the glass. Poor Sarajane looked positively

stricken. Could this be the wrong music? She glanced at the empty tape box. Yes, it was number 4. But in the rush to speak to Araminta after Toby's warning, might she have slid it in on the wrong side?

Oh, no! Toby would kill her when he realized there was something wrong. In desperate hope, Bonny held on for one or two more bars, in case the thunder came. But it was hopeless. It didn't sound at all the right sort of music for rushing round being a raindrop. Clearly the only thing to do was take out the tape and start again. Sarajane looked more and more panicked as the wrong music poured out behind her. And a great scowl was gathering on Toby's face.

Bonny's finger reached out for the STOP button. But just at that moment, Sarajane threw back her head and opened her mouth wide. Bonny hesitated. Had she decided to press on and sing whatever it was she had recorded on the other side?

The haunting melody rose. And out of Sarajane's mouth there poured a waterfall of notes so pure and lovely that Bonny's hand froze from sheer enchantment.

'Dark my days, and dark my hours
Since Lord Henry broke my heart.
I'll forsake these golden bowers
And the seas of grief I'll chart.'

Beside her, Toby moved closer to the glass. Already the glower on his face had cleared. He looked entranced, and Bonny could see the fingers on his left hand twitching, as though, as he listened, he was playing the melody along with his precious Sarajane on some imaginary violin.

The glorious voice poured out of the loud-speakers. Even Araminta had put down the bucket and stopped looking wistful as she listened.

'Lost my hopes, and lost my beauty
Since Lord Henry rode away.
Was there ever such a cruelty?
Was there ever such dismay?'

The lovely voice soared. Even if Toby weren't in the way, rapt and unreachable, there was no need for Bonny to switch on any glittering showers. Sarajane's voice alone

could glitter and sparkle, flash and blaze. All Bonny had to do was keep the simple spotlight trained on her. If she could sing like this and steal their hearts, why should she bother even to step out of the bright circle of light that was all Bonny offered?

> *'Will Lord Henry hear my singing?*
> *Shall I charm him back to me,*
> *In his ears, my verses ringing,*
> *In his heart, my melody?'*

The music swelled and died. The song was over. Sarajane hung her head, deeply embarrassed, and, for a moment or two, there was no sound at all.

Beside Bonny, Toby stirred uneasily. Beyond the glass, the clapping started. Araminta put the bucket back where it was supposed to be, and Mrs Opalene dabbed at her eyes with a frilly lace handkerchief.

Toby's eyes shifted to the audience.

'Whose is that spare seat next to Sarajane's?'

'It's Araminta's. She's not using it.'

Instantly, he was at the door. 'Silly to waste it.'

'You're soft on Sarajane, aren't you?'

Did he even hear her? She didn't think so. He'd already gone. Bonny sighed heavily. And after all those lofty speeches about silly girls! (Though, to be fair, he'd stuck with just feeling soft until he'd heard her singing so beautifully. It was her talent, not her pretty face, that had bewitched his heart.)

As he slipped into Araminta's empty seat, Mrs Opalene rose from her own overfull one.

'My dearest Sarajane,' she said, still plainly moved. 'That was *incomparable*.'

Nobody knew what incomparable meant. But it was obvious it was a compliment of the highest order, so everyone happily nodded along. And, after that, it was quite clear to them that Mrs Opalene was almost as taken with the new-style Curls and Purls Show as her pupils.

'Memorable, dear! Memorable!' she said, enchanted, after Lulu's 'cowboy sweetheart' song, when Araminta popped up behind the cardboard stockade wearing the bison horns she'd found in the stockroom, and Bonny turned on the tornado and sent tumbleweed bouncing across the prairie backdrop.

'Exotic!' she marvelled after the firework explosions that shook the stage all through Cristalle's lullaby.

'Rivetingly tasteless, dear,' was her judgement after Angelica's *Beauty and her Mirror* song, during which Bonny fiddled with the lighting until Angelica aged horribly before their eyes, then turned into a skull.

'Disquietingly vertiginous,' she said faintly when Araminta's own turn finally came round, and Bonny made the snowflakes swirl so fast that Araminta finally got dizzy and fell over.

And how Bonny managed to turn Cooki's pretty fairy ring of mushrooms into that waterlogged swamp of crocodiles, Mrs Opalene swore she'd never know.

At last it was over. Cindy-Lou swatted out fiercely one last time at all the shadow bats that had so mysteriously swooped in to join her gracious *Tea-time with the Vicar* mime. Down came the curtain, and Mrs Opalene sailed up the stairs and stood on the stage apron.

'Well, dears!' she declared. 'That was ...'

And, for the first time in her life, Mrs Opalene was lost for words.

'Such *fun*,' said Araminta, coming out of the wings, and hugging Mrs Opalene. 'Such wonderful fun!'

'Marvellous!' called out Lulu.

'Fabulous!'

'Terrific!'

Pearl hugged herself. 'It was,' she breathed in ecstasy, 'the very best Curls and Purls Show *ever*!'

Mrs Opalene capitulated graciously. 'Yes, dears. I do agree it made the most amusing and interesting change. And we must certainly think of doing it that way again some other time.'

'Not just some other time, Mrs Opalene! *Next* time!'

'Not just *next* time, Mrs Opalene! *Every* time!'

Mrs Opalene looked down at them, startled. Where were the modest and amenable girls with whom she'd spent the morning? Sitting in front of her now were a crowd of smudged, untidy urchins, fidgeting and grinning, and calling out, uncurbed.

'Now, girls!' she reproved them. 'Aren't we beginning to forget that we try to stay very best friends with Miss Manners?'

At the words, 'very best friends', Araminta swivelled in her seat and blew a sparkling, Araminta-ish kiss at Bonny through the glass.

Bonny had never blown a kiss before. Like lots of other things in Charm School that day, it was a first. She blew it back while Mrs Opalene went on with her lecture. 'In fact, dears, as you know, ladies *never* shout out like this when they want something. They simply think of a roundabout way of suggesting it nicely, in the hope that—'

But no-one was listening.

'Mrs Opalene!' Pearl's voice rose over the

others. 'That was such fun that I don't think I could go back to doing it the old way. There was just too much sitting around and waiting. And watching everyone else mince up and down looking pretty was boring too.' She sighed wistfully. 'I had such *fun* today. Amethyst was *brilliant*. I wish I could act like that.' Suddenly, a thought struck her. 'Do they do acting classes here, as well?'

Some of those listening couldn't help noticing there was a shade of bitterness in Bonny's voice as it came through the loudspeaker. 'Yes, there are acting classes, but they don't start till next week.'

Once again, Mrs Opalene found herself facing unladylike chaos.

'Acting!'

'Yes!'

'Oh, I'd *adore* to learn to act!'

'And are there painting classes, too? If there were, I'd go to them. Then I could paint Amethyst an even *creepier* forest backdrop.'

'Saturdays,' Bonny informed Suki. 'Two till four. Bring your own paints.'

'Sarajane should take singing. Or choir. If I had a voice as lovely as hers, I wouldn't want to waste it.'

'Tuesdays, at six.'

'I've always wanted to learn juggling, personally.'

'Thursdays, from January till April.'

'Did you see the tornado? And the prairie? And the swamp full of crocodiles? I'd love to know more about those sorts of things.'

'Natural geography,' Bonny informed her through the loudspeakers. 'On Wednesdays at lunchtime, repeated Friday nights.'

Mrs Opalene saw her class melting away before her eyes.

'Girls! Girls!' she said. 'Perhaps Pearl's right. Maybe it would be nice to—' she wondered how to put it '—*broaden out* a little.'

'What? Learn a few other things? Like how to work the lights, and the sound?'

'And make people laugh?'

'And tell jokes?'

'And juggle!'

'Excellent! In that case, I'll certainly be coming back.'

'Me, too!'

'And me.'

Mrs Opalene looked thrilled. 'Really, dears? Oh, I'm so pleased. And maybe, over time, we'll get to find extra things to interest *everyone*.'

A dreamy look spread over Cooki's face. 'I'll tell you what interested me. Those astonishing fireworks. They were *breathtaking*!'

'*My* breath,' Cristalle reminded her. 'I was so terrified, I could hardly finish my lullaby.'

'Oh, but they looked so *real*. I *loved* them.' The dreamy look sharpened. 'Do you suppose that we could broaden out enough to learn how to make fireworks, Mrs Opalene?'

Mrs Opalene blanched. 'No, dear. I don't think so. I fear, if we took up with flashes and explosions, we'd end up stepping on Dr Hooper's toes.'

'Who's Dr Hooper?'

'Chemistry,' Bonny informed them. 'Tuesdays, at five.' She couldn't help adding, with the tinge of bitterness they'd all come to recognize, 'But that's another class that doesn't start till September.'

'That's fine. I'll wait,' said Cooki. 'Do you want to come with me, Angelica?'

'No.' Angelica was adamant. 'I'm definitely off to do Geography.'

How odd, thought Bonny, still in the control room. Only this morning they'd have been wishing one another away sick in bed, or off on holiday, so there'd be fewer of them out

to win the glistering tiara. Now they were asking one another to come along to these new classes – even the ones who hadn't seemed good friends before.

'Lulu? Will you come?'

Lulu was torn. 'The fireworks were lovely. But, no. I'm still going to choose painting.'

Mrs Opalene looked crestfallen. Suki consoled her. 'Never mind. You mustn't worry. You'll still have plenty of people. Because, now we won't just be walking in boring old beauty all the time, a lot of our friends will probably start coming too.'

Mrs Opalene clasped her hands eagerly. 'Oh, do you think so?'

'I'm sure so. Now that we won't be spending all our time suffering to be beautiful.'

Cooki looked up. 'If we don't have to suffer to get in those frocks all the time, then I'll come back to Charm School as well as Chemistry.' Under her breath, she added mischievously, '*And* I'll have two slices of pizza, if I'm hungry!'

'I'll carry on coming as well!'

'Me, too!'

'And me!'

Mrs Opalene cheered up. 'Well, dears,' she

said. 'Perhaps it's all for the best. I have been
giving these classes for years and years. And
times do change. If you're all busy doing all
these other interesting things, you simply
won't have quite so much time to sit with
your elbows in lemon halves, and wander
round the shops looking for just the right
thing.'

Her eye fell on Toby, holding Sarajane's
hand.

'Though I do hope, whatever you're all busy
doing, you'll always try and remember how to
behave.'

A thought struck Araminta suddenly.

'Won't we have to change the Charm School
motto, now we won't be suffering any more?'

Mrs Opalene looked anxious. 'Oh, dear!
Oh, dear!'

'I know!' cried Lulu. 'How about,
Handsome is as Handsome does?'

'What about, *Beauty is in the eye of the
Beholder?*' called out Esmeralda.

'I quite like, *Beauty is Truth, Truth
Beauty,*' quoted Cooki.

Horrified, Mrs Opalene put up her hand to
stem the rising tide of heresy. 'Shall we leave
that till later, dears? For the moment, let's

just decide who we're going to crown the Supreme Queen, and then we'll do all these other things next time.'

Next time! Bonny looked round at the chaos in the control room and wondered what on earth the famous Maura would think of all the mess when she came back. Leaping off her swivel chair, she hastily started putting things away in boxes. She didn't want Maura complaining to Mrs Opalene. Mrs Opalene might not be keen to have her back.

And she might want to come. After all, if Charm School was, as she hoped, about to turn into Fun School, it would be a wonderful way of spending time with Araminta. Though they might even turn out to be in the same school... In the same class, even! Thinking how wonderful this would be, Bonny stuffed one slide and stencil and cassette after another into what she hoped were the right places. She was still busy putting things away when Araminta burst in.

'Ah!' Bonny joked. 'Just the person I need. Miss Tidy by Nature!'

But Araminta wasn't listening. Rushing to a little cabinet on the wall, she unlocked it, and carefully drew out a beautiful sparkling

tiara set on a flat satin cushion spangled with shimmering crystal beads.

Holding it reverently, she walked past Bonny, busy on her knees, and carried it back to Mrs Opalene.

Mrs Opalene held it high.

'I wish there was one for everybody,' she said. 'You all gave such fine performances. It's so hard to decide. And we never even got round to doing the catwalk parade, which might have helped me choose the winner properly.'

'We could still do that now,' suggested Angelica.

Mrs Opalene looked down at them all, and shuddered. 'I don't think so, dears. You all look a little bit—' the word was 'scruffy', but it seemed so rude '—*unpolished*. And I'm afraid I somehow mislaid my marking pad while that frightful wolverine was growling at Amethyst. So, dears, I'm horribly afraid I'm not quite sure who ought to be—'

But Araminta was on her feet again in her excitement.

'It's obvious, Mrs Opalene! There's someone here who's won it fair and square. Amethyst made us scream with terror, stuck in that awful forest. And Serena made us laugh ourselves silly, tumbling into that well. And Sarajane made us cry with her beautiful singing.' In the interests of honesty, she amended this. 'Well, *some* of us,' she added politely. 'But who made all of us do it?'

They were silent. In their heart of hearts, every single one of them knew that, but for one person, at this very moment they'd have been mincing up and down the catwalk in their pretty frocks, trying to look beautiful enough to win the glistering tiara. And instead of bouncing up and down excitedly on their seats, as they were now, making interesting plans for the future, all except one of them would have gone home and sobbed into her pillows, feeling nothing but clumsy, or podgy, or ugly.

It was a struggle. But they'd had a brilliant afternoon. And there were good times to come.

'All right. That's fair enough.'

'Yes. I agree.'

'She did a *spectacular* show.'

'Those bats!'

'Those *rats*!'

'Personally, I loved the tumbleweed. Do you suppose I should be thinking of classes in Botany?'

Deep in her boxes, Bonny overheard the word 'Botany' coming through the sound system. 'Mondays,' she called out automatically. 'Between six and eight, with optional Saturday field trips.'

Once again, Mrs Opalene had visions of a vanishing class.

'Right, then,' she said hastily. 'Since you obviously all agree, the glistering tiara goes to—'

Everyone shouted it together.

'Miss Sparky!'

Startled, Bonny looked up from her tidying.

'What?'

'Miss Sparky!' Mrs Opalene called out again. 'Our own Supreme Queen! Time to be crowned, dear, with our lovely glistering tiara.'

All the blood drained from Bonny's face.

'Oh, no! Oh, no!'

Staying on all fours, she made for the door. The knees of her jeans picked up huge dusty smudges, but she didn't care. She just kept her head down and carried on scuttling towards the huge green glowing sign that promised EXIT.

Two leggy pillars suddenly barred her way. Toby.

'And where do you think you're going?'

'Home!' Bonny whispered. 'Quickly! Before they get me!'

'They're not planning on *hanging* you,' Toby pointed out. 'They simply want to make you Supreme Queen.'

'Well, it's *ridiculous*.'

'No, it isn't.'

'Yes, it is!'

'Well,' Toby said judiciously. 'I do agree it is a *little* strange that you should be the winner.' A soppy smile spread over his face. 'I mean, it is a bit difficult to see how anyone could have chosen you after that touching and heart-rending song about Lord Henry—'

'Excuse *me*,' Bonny interrupted tartly. 'But if it weren't for me, your precious Sarajane would have sung a song that goes, "Drip, drip, drip".'

'But that was just your mistake.'

He was quite right, of course. But he'd annoyed her. For a moment she couldn't think of any suitable retort. And then Mrs Opalene's words came back to her, about reaching the heights of fashion. And she told him loftily, 'On the contrary. It was a combination of vision, and planning, and hard, hard work.'

He looked impressed. 'Oh, well,' he said. 'In that case, fair enough. After all, Sarajane probably has a whole lifetime of singing prizes in front of her.' He blushed. 'In fact, she says she's going to let me accompany her on my violin. So, now I *really* need a better one, I won't mind doing this boring job so much each Saturday.'

'If Mrs Opalene's classes go the way I think they're going,' Bonny said, 'your job won't be so boring in future.'

'True.' He looked delighted. 'Well, then,' he said. 'You seem to have sorted out just about everybody in one short day. I definitely think that you deserve the glistering tiara.'

Bonny thought about it for a moment. She looked at all the lamps and equipment she'd worked so hard to learn how to handle, so

they could have their brilliant show. And she thought of the changes she'd made for them. And she thought of Araminta.

'Yes,' she agreed. 'I think that I deserve it, too. I've earned it fair and square. I'll wear it with pride.'

'Good,' Toby said. 'And Sarajane can be crowned with my admiration instead.'

'That's nice,' said Bonny. 'She'll look good in that.' And, laughing, she walked out as Toby opened the door for her, bowing like a footman.

Everyone was waiting. Mrs Opalene beamed. 'Ah, there you are, dear! It is a pity we don't have time to dress you up a bit, just for the presentation. You would have looked such a treat in Cindy-Lou's Blushing Rose frock. But, never mind. We must just make the best of things.'

Obligingly, Bonny dusted the knees of her jeans before walking up the steps.

Mrs Opalene held the glistering tiara aloft. Its rhinestones sparkled and the sequins sewn onto its velvet rim twinkled in the gleam of the one spotlight Bonny hadn't yet switched off.

'It gives me *inordinate* pleasure,' said Mrs

Opalene, 'to place this precious crowning glory onto the head of our most deserving Supreme Queen: *Miss Sparky*!'

None of them knew what inordinate meant. But they cheered anyway as Mrs Opalene wedged the tiara firmly on the unruly hedge of Bonny's hair, and Cindy-Lou took a photo.

'There, dear! Don't you look nice?'

Bonny could see from her reflection in every mirror round the room that hers would be the first of all the photographs in the corridor outside to show a grimy face with unbrushed hair wearing the prized tiara.

Her look of triumph, though, would fit in very well.

'Thank you,' she told them all. 'Thank you. I've had a wonderful day. I can't remember when I last had so much fun. I'm really glad I chose to come to Charm School.'

'Are you, dear?'

Mrs Opalene was *thrilled*.

Bonny couldn't help hugging her. 'Yes. Yes, I am. And I'll be back again next time, if you'll let me.'

'My dear, we'll be honoured,' Mrs Opalene said. 'Honoured and *charmed*.'

The rest of the afternoon passed in a flash of tidying, and laughing, and swapping jokes and stories, and putting away chairs, and exchanging phone numbers and addresses. It seemed to Bonny it was half an hour at most before Mrs Opalene finally ushered the last of them out into the corridor and along to the lift.

'Bye, dears! Take good care! See you all next time!'

'Bye, Mrs Opalene! Bye!'

On the ground floor, Bonny spilled out of the lift, giggling, surrounded by chattering girls. Beside the desk, Mrs Bramble stood holding her certificate, and talking to the lady who had sold them their tickets. Both of them stared as Bonny rushed over to greet them.

Neither could understand how that sour and resentful creature from whom they'd parted that morning could have turned into the bubbling, excited person in front of them now.

'Mum! Mum! Come and meet Minty!' She pointed round the group of girls. 'And Cooki! And Lulu! And Esmeralda! And Cindy-Lou! And—'

Mrs Bramble waved her certificate in Bonny's face. Snatching it, Bonny inspected her mother's name on the dotted line, then hugged her proudly. 'You did it! Brilliant! Well done!'

'What about you?' asked Mrs Bramble. And then, unable to deny the evidence of Bonny's shining eyes, and all the girls gathering round her, she risked the tiniest little tease.

'A little bit better than you expected, was it?'

Bonny's face was radiant. 'Better? It was *brilliant*! I learned so much, and made so many friends. I even won their funny old glistering tiara, and I'm Miss Sparky for a whole year! And Minty's going to phone me tonight – if the phone's on yet. And, Mum, can I come back again next time Mrs Opalene runs

Charm School? Oh, please, please, *please*! I'll help unpack all the packing crates, and sort out the plates and dishes, and put things away in cupboards, and—'

She reached for her mother's basket.

'Oh, let me carry all those heavy accounting books. You must be tired. I'll take these to the car.'

Mrs Bramble stared at her daughter. What on earth had happened all day up there on the third floor? What on earth was the glistering tiara? How would you get to be a Miss Sparky? And who was this Mrs Opalene, who'd weaved such magic over the miserable, sullen daughter she'd been arguing with that morning?

No time to ask now. Already Bonny was frantically waving and calling to a couple leaving arm in arm. 'Bye, Toby! Bye, Sarajane!' In fact, she didn't stop waving and calling out her merry goodbyes to her new friends till they were safely in the car.

Mrs Bramble could hardly believe it.

Only one day at Charm School.

But it worked.

♥190♥

Miss Sparky

Now flip the book
to read

Bad Dreams

★ ☀ ♥ ☆

Now flip the book
to read

Charm School

★ ☀ ♥ ☆

Frozen Billy

ANNE FINE

Could a stage dummy have the
power to destroy a family?

Clarrie and Will live with their Uncle Len —
a brilliant ventriloquist in the nearby
music hall. But though Len loves his act
almost as much as he loves his beer,
Top Billing is out of his grasp until Will
thinks up a way to double the drama with
a new act and some extraordinary new
patter that he and Frozen Billy
can share on stage.

It s a grand idea, hatched in hope and
excitement. But, to Clarrie s horror, soon it
begins to turn terribly sour . . .

DOUBLEDAY
0 385 60769 5

Serena turned her back to brush an invisible speck of dust from one of the frills on her frock.

Bonny seized the moment. 'Quick, Araminta!' she whispered through the only microphone still on SOUND OUT. 'Push the well over the trapdoor.'

Araminta dashed on the stage and pushed the cardboard well a few inches over. Then she glanced up at Bonny at the controls and put her thumbs up.

'Dear!' Mrs Opalene called. 'Shouldn't you be down here, in your seat?'

Araminta flashed Mrs Opalene one of her stunning, star-spangled smiles. 'I was just helping out a little,' she explained, 'because you've always said how very important it is to be as helpful as you can.' And she dashed off between the drapes into the wings, before Mrs Opalene could argue.

Serena turned back and gave the audience her prettiest smile. With her marking pencil in her hand, Mrs Opalene gave her a little wave.

'As soon as you're ready, dear ...'

Serena nodded at Bonny through the glass, and Bonny slid the first tape into the cassette

player. After a moment's silence, in which
Serena's set smile gradually began to freeze,
out came a swell of violins, playing a sickly
tune.

Serena sprang to life.
Pressing the back of her
hand against her fore-
head she began her
song.

> 'My earring! My earring! I have lost it down
>   the well.
> I reached over for the bucket, and into the
>   depths it fell.
> Oh, what am I to do now? I am stricken! I
>   am sad!
> For my earrings were a present from a
>   handsome, charming lad.'

At this point, Serena began to twirl, while
heavenly choirs on the tape kept up the chorus without her.

> 'Her earring! Her earring! She has lost it
>   down the well.
> Will her love survive this dreadful shock?
> Not one of us can tell.'

Following Serena's instructions, Bonny turned up the drum rolls. Serena pressed her dainty fingertips to her temple and started on the second verse.

'If he peeps, he'll see it twinkle. If he peers, he'll see it flash.
And perhaps he will be angry, and away from me he'll dash.
He may fall in love with Flora from the farm along the way,
And I'll spend my whole life sobbing at the well-side. Lackaday!'

In the control room, Bonny whispered, 'Go!' Again, Araminta put her thumbs up, then, draping one of the fluffy white blankets they'd found in the storeroom tightly round her shoulders, she crept on all fours like a baby sheep, closer and closer to Serena, who was too busy twirling through the chorus to notice her.

Bonny's fingers were tingling with excitement over the switch labelled STAGE TRAPDOOR. As Serena embarked on the last verse, she waited for Araminta's little 'baa-aa' as a signal, then flicked it from CLOSED to

OPEN. Serena's song rang out quite loud enough to hide the low, mechanical rumble as the trapdoor slid open beneath the cardboard well.

> 'Since I know my love will leave me, and my
> tears I cannot quell,
> In the darkness of despair and deepest mis-
> ery I'll dwell.

In a dramatic gesture of grief, Serena raised herself on tiptoe and spread her arms. Just at that moment, Bonny pressed the two buttons labelled LIGHTNING FLASH and THUNDERCLAP, and Araminta the blanketed lambkin scuttled forward and butted Serena hard. Momentarily blinded by lightning, none of the audience saw. And deafened by thunder, none of them heard Serena's startled scream as, losing her balance totally, she dropped her beribboned crook and toppled out of sight into the well in a flurry of white bloomers.

But everyone heard the splash when she fell headfirst in the water bucket Bonny and Araminta had, giggling merrily, put underneath the trap door earlier.

Serena came up dripping just in time to hear the impostor sheep singing two new last lines to her song.

'And to maidens the world over the sad news this sheep will tell –
How she's gone to join her earrings at the bottom of the well!'

Everyone cheered. Some of them, it must be admitted, were just delighted because Serena looked so terrible, with ringlets like rats' tails and eyes smudged as black as coal holes. But all the others had very much enjoyed the song, with the excitement of the sheep creeping closer to Serena, the *flash!* and *bang!*, and the ungainly tumble down the well.

'Well done, Serena!'

'That was brilliant!'

Serena made a parting in her dripping hair, so she could peer out. Everyone was laughing and clapping. She stood a moment, wondering whether to giggle or cry. And then, deciding it would be a whole lot smarter to make the best of things, she spread her hands modestly.

'I just thought you'd all like something a little different,' she said. 'And it was *fun.*'

Everyone looked at Mrs Opalene, to see what she made of this change of plan. But, though she looked rather dubious, and anyone could tell she wasn't very much at ease with Serena's tangled wet hair and ruined make-up, she was still Mrs Opalene, and couldn't help saying something nice.

'Very—' She hesitated. 'Very *authentic,* dear!'

Not knowing what authentic meant, Serena took it for a compliment, and smiled very prettily all the way back down the stairs to her seat.

Araminta waved frantically at Bonny and pointed to the microphone.

Bonny switched to SOUND IN.

'You were right!' Araminta whispered excitedly. 'Mrs Opalene is *enjoying* it. She *did* want a change.'

She didn't have time to say more because Mrs Opalene was already calling, 'Next!'

Esmeralda was next. Smoothing her slinky green skirt, she took her place on the stage. In her bright yellow top, with matching petal hat, she looked exactly as she'd planned, like

a willowy spring flower. Bonny flicked switches till the stage took on a sunlit hue. She wound down the backdrop Esmeralda wanted – another country scene – and dropped special effects sheets into the slots of the lanterns. Across the stage appeared a sprinkling of yellow dots, like a rash of spring flowers. And spinning across the painted blue sky were a host of puffy white clouds.

'*The Buttercup Song*,' declared Esmeralda. Waving her body from side to side, she started off.

> '*Gentle country breezes*
> *Sway me to and fro,*
> *Kiss me and caress me,*
> *And make me lovely grow.*'

In the control room, Bonny switched on a tape of sounds labelled 'Weather'. And, in the wings, Araminta turned the knob of Maura's wind machine on to BREEZE.

On the stage, Esmeralda's petal hat lifted and fluttered prettily. But on she sang.

> '*Lovely winds of heaven*
> *Raise my petals high*

To keep me ever busy
Worshipping the sky.'

Bonny forwarded the weather tape on to
'Very windy', and Araminta turned the wind
machine up a notch to match. Esmeralda
looked startled as her petals flapped violent-
ly. Clutching the rim of her hat, she raised
her voice above the gathering sound and
embarked on her third verse.

'Fearful storms of winter
Shall not come my way.
Safe and warm I stand here
On this mild spring day.'

Araminta winked at Bonny through a gap
in the side drapes and both of them, giggling,
turned up to STORM. One by one, all of
Esmeralda's petals tore from her hat and flew
off into the wings. Esmeralda was horrified.
But Mrs Opalene was still staring kindly, if a
little bemusedly, in her direction. And one of
the things she always said over and over was,
'The worst thing you can do on stage is stop.
Whatever happens, dears, press on. Press
on!'

So, bravely gripping the last remaining shreds of hat rim, Esmeralda sang on.

'What care I for tempests?
I shall have no fear.
A proud and yellow buttercup,
Simple flower of cheer.'

On the last note, Bonny and Araminta switched up to TEMPEST. Instantly both halves of Esmeralda's little buttercup outfit ripped off and swirled away into the wings. Determined not to fail at the last minute, Esmeralda resolutely bawled out the last verse in her vest and knickers.

'See me in my beauty!
Watch me in my pride!
A glorious golden buttercup,
Springtime's happy bride!'

Still grinning at one another, Bonny and Araminta switched to OFF. Just for a moment, Bonny feared there might have been some electrical fault because out in the big room the noise seemed to be carrying on without fading. But then she realized it was all the others, roaring their approval.

♥153♥

'Esmeralda, that was the funniest thing I've ever seen!'

'Brilliant!'

'You're so clever, keeping it a secret till the show!'

'You never told us you were so good at comedy skits!'

While they were all applauding, long and loud, Araminta rushed round the back of the stage and lifted Esmeralda's slinky green skirt off the lantern from which it was dangling. She ran on stage and handed it to Esmeralda, who hugged it to her body and proudly took bow after bow. Then, nervously, Esmeralda looked at Mrs Opalene.

Mrs Opalene's lips pursed. On the one hand, here was a girl with blown-about hair standing unashamedly on a stage in her underwear. But on the other hand, everyone was cheering frenziedly, and she did so want all of her girls to be happy.

'Well, dear,' said Mrs Opalene at last, choosing her words with care. 'That was a shade outlandish, I confess. But I think everyone enjoyed it thoroughly.'

Esmeralda beamed. She wasn't sure quite what outlandish meant. But she knew about

enjoying things thoroughly. Especially warm applause. In fact, she wouldn't mind trying the song all over again sometime soon. She could do it even better. She could put in some of those silly faces she made to amuse her baby sister. And she could rewrite the words of the song so it was a weather forecaster standing there. That would be even funnier. Or she could—

'Next!' called Mrs Opalene firmly.

Amethyst floated up the steps onto the stage, flicked her hair and stood shyly in her glorious silver gown, cradling a glittering wand. She couldn't help feeling a little bit more nervous than usual. The other two had had such very exciting acts. They'd been such fun to watch. And all she had was … Well, never mind. What Mrs Opalene always said was, 'Don't waste time wishing yourself like other people. Just make the best of what you have.'

What she had was pretty unexciting. But she'd make the very best of it.

'I'm going to perform *The Dance of the Evening Star*,' she explained to them carefully. 'I'm going to be Starlight. As evening falls around me, I wake and flutter to and fro, touching the wonders of nature lightly with

my starry wand.' She waved it, to show them. 'And everything glistens with starlight, just for me, because everything loves me so much.'

In the control room Bonny shook her head in amazement that anyone would willingly dance something so soppy. She couldn't imagine anything more likely to banish any lingering doubts she might have had that she was doing Mrs Opalene's girls a giant favour, sparking up their Curls and Purls Show.

'Anyway,' went on Amethyst, 'I dance all night, except that, obviously, in the dance, the night only lasts two minutes. Then I curl up in my forest dell and fall asleep. And daybreak comes. Then I wake up and flee.'

'Lovely!' said Mrs Opalene, filled with relief that one of her precious girls, at least, was planning something more ladylike and traditional. 'Lovely, dear Amethyst! I do so look forward to seeing how very elegantly you can flee.'

Amethyst smiled. Her beautiful face lit up. 'Yes,' she admitted. 'I have been practising fleeing.' She turned to face the glass window and nodded at Bonny, who slid in music tape number 3, and wound down the forest backdrop Amethyst had chosen earlier.

'Creepy!' admired Bonny. 'Like when you shine a torch through your fingers.'

Araminta switched from the backlight to a lamp tucked between the side drapes. 'And now she's sidelit. She has half a face.'

'Like an eclipse.'

'Interesting,' said Araminta. 'But not what we want.' She flicked another switch. 'And neither is this,' she said sternly.

Suddenly Pearl looked bony and ill.

'How did you do that?' said Bonny. 'She looks *terrible*. She looks as if she just crawled out of her grave.'

'That's lighting her from underneath. It is about the cruellest thing that you can do, and if you try it on me, I shall break off your arm, and beat you to death with the soggy end.'

'Charming!'

'Oh, dear!' Araminta clapped her hands over her mouth and looked shocked with herself.

Bonny just grinned. 'I still think it's brilliant,' she said. 'Absolutely *brilliant*.'

'But I'm not singing a monster song,' Araminta reproved her. 'I'm being a pretty snowflake, don't forget.' She looked a little wistful. 'Though it would be fun ...'

Very fast, one by one, she flicked more switches. And by turns, one by one, Pearl went all grey and ghostly, then burst out again with rosy health, then turned so shadowy and sinister that she sent shivers down Bonny's spine.

'That is *amazing*!' breathed Bonny when Pearl's skin changed to pale green before her eyes, and Araminta somehow turned the boards under her feet into shimmering silver wave patterns. 'Show me again!'

'You'd better not do anything like this to me,' warned Araminta. 'What I want is this.' She pressed down a whole row of switches. Suddenly Pearl looked as luminous as an angel, with her skin all milky and glowing.

'Now she even *looks* like a pearl!'

'Yes, but watch this.' Araminta slid two of the controls up in their runnels till Pearl's face was transfigured with a soft pink blush.

'How did you *do* that?' breathed Bonny, mesmerized.

Araminta showed her again.

'That's what *I* want,' she said. 'But, don't forget, around me I must have a swirling snowstorm.' She dived into one of the boxes on the floor and drew out a plastic disc. 'No,

that's not the right one,' she said, holding it up to the light. 'That's rain spatters on a pond. Where are the snowflakes?'

She rooted again, tugging out what she wanted. 'Here it is!' Bonny watched as she dropped it neatly into the slot in one of the lanterns, and flicked a switch to start it revolving.

'Look!'

Bonny swung round to the stage again. Poor Pearl was standing in a raging blizzard.

'Whoops! Too fast!' said Araminta, twisting a knob to settle the blizzard into a gentle swirl of fat white flakes. 'There! That's nice.'

'It's *wonderful!*' said Bonny. 'It's astonishing! I think you're the cleverest person I ever saw. You've got magic at a touch and the world at your fingertips.'

Araminta's eyes shone. 'If you think I'm good, you should see Maura in action. Maura can conjure up thunderstorms and set off avalanches. She can make sheets of lava bubble out of the tops of volcanoes, and thin coils of smoke trail up from chimneypots. She can send tumbleweed bouncing across the prairie and tornadoes spinning through cornfields. She can turn a baking desert into a flood, and a flood back into a desert.'

'All at the flick of a switch!'

Araminta spun round on her toes. 'Full moon. New moon.'

'High tide. Low tide.'

'Golden dawn. Blue dusk.'

'Bright day. Black night.'

'And then there's the sound! She has *everything*. Roaring winds. Birdsong. Car crashes!'

Hands locked together, they were both

spinning now, faster and faster. When Bonny narrowed her eyes, all she could see was Araminta in a swirl of glittering white.

'Brass bands. Heavenly choirs.'
'Gunshots. Explosions.'
'Children outside in the playground.'
'Breaking glass.'
'A baby whimpering.'
'Crashing surf.'
'A piano in a far-off room.'
'Trains hurtling past.'

'Church bells. Whistling kettles.'

'Street riots. Sirens. Crackling fires.'

Dizzy, they slowed to a halt, still holding hands. 'You must be mad,' said Bonny. 'You must be absolutely crazy.'

'Crazy?' Araminta looked baffled, and very hurt.

'Yes.' Somehow, Bonny couldn't help saying it. 'Crazy.' All of her earlier disappointment had swept back, and worse. All the long journey in the car alone with her mother she'd hoped so much that, in this strange new town, she'd find a friend – someone as sunny and sparkling and wonderful as Araminta. And now she'd found her. But, to keep her by her side, she'd have to spend at least half of her life drivelling on about things like five-strand bracelets and silver-pink nail polish, and whether flower earrings had somehow suddenly become 'Totally Yesterday' between last Wednesday and this Friday.

And it was such an awful waste of time. Too high a price to pay. So she tried yet again to explain to Araminta. 'Listen. It doesn't make *sense*. Here you are, with the chance to do all these amazing things, and build whole worlds around you. You could sit in that swivel

chair and flick switches to frighten people out of their wits, or lull them to sleep with soft music. You have the power to do *anything*.' She spread her hands and stared at Araminta. 'And what do you choose to do?'

And then, in her exasperation and frustration, she startled herself by answering her own question rudely. 'You just choose to sit on your bum and hope you look prettier than everyone around you!'

Tears sprang to Araminta's eyes and glittered like the shawl. 'That is so horrible! And so *unfair*.'

Bonny felt terrible. But still, instead of saying she was sorry, she muttered sullenly, 'What's so unfair about it? Isn't it true?'

'No! No, it's *not*!' Araminta glared through her tears and cast round for some way of hurting Bonny back. 'And you're only saying it because you're jealous.'

Now this was irritating. '*Jealous?*'

'Of course!' Araminta curled her lip. 'You're only being horrible because you know that never in a million years could someone like you win Mrs Opalene's beautiful glistering tiara!'

Bonny said scornfully, 'And what on earth

would someone like me want with some stupid, blistering tiara?'

The colour rushed to Araminta's cheeks. 'Oh, right! Nothing!' She took a deep breath, and rushed on. 'Because it certainly wouldn't look right on someone with your cheap, raggedy-looking haircut, and your dull face, and those jeans that do absolutely *nothing* for your figure!'

'Because I prefer to spend the hours of my life actually living, and not just waste them fussing about every silly square inch of my body?' Bonny said loftily.

'And it shows!'

'Who's being horrible now?' taunted Bonny.

Araminta went scarlet with frustration. 'You started it!' she practically screamed. 'You said that I was *crazy*.'

Bonny knew only too well that this was her last chance to back down. And maybe she would have tried to make up again with Araminta. But, looking away for a moment, she caught sight of Pearl, still patiently standing waiting in the middle of the stage, her face quite blank, and, for all Bonny knew, her mind quite blank as well.

Oh, they were all the same, these silly,

silly, *empty* girls.

'And so you are! Quite crazy!' she ended up shouting back in her impatience. 'Sitting for hours in that lolly-dolly circle, with daft Mrs Opalene, learning about cucumber slices and oatmeal face packs.'

She'd gone too far, insulting gentle, friendly Mrs Opalene. Instantly, Araminta sprang to her beloved teacher's defence.

'It's better than being—'

She broke off. And Bonny knew she ought to let it go. But something made her push Araminta into saying it, like some tired, miserable toddler who, not allowed to have the toy she wants, breaks the one that she's holding.

'What?' she asked dangerously. 'Better than being *what*?'

'Nothing,' snapped Araminta.

'Go on! Spit it out!' jeered Bonny.

And Araminta cracked. 'All right!' she shouted. 'You're snooty and mean about all of us, and horrid about dear Mrs Opalene. So I *will* say it! It's better than being a nasty little scruffpot with no looks at all!'

They stared at one another, shocked, their fresh new friendship in tatters.

'Oh, go away!' said Bonny, close to tears. 'Go back to your pretty little circle and learn something really important, like how to moisturize between your toes.'

Forgetting her shawl in her upset, Araminta rushed to the door and wrenched it open.

'You act so superior,' she hissed. 'But if it didn't mean we'd have to have you back in the class, I'd tell Mrs Opalene right now that you're nothing but a *fake*. You go round so sure you know how everybody else ought to live. But you ought to try looking in a mirror. It's obvious you don't bother to do it very often, but you *should*, because you'll see something really interesting.'

'Oh, yes?' said Bonny icily. 'And what's that?'

'I'll tell you!' shouted Araminta. 'Oh, yes. I'll tell you! I absolutely guarantee that, staring back at you out of that mirror, you'll see—'

She darted forward. Down went her pretty painted fingertips to push up the volume and flick on the echo switch before she finished up triumphantly,

'—the meanest girl I ever saw!'

Round flew the echoes, round and round,
bouncing off walls and curdling the air.

'The meanest girl I ever saw!'

'Ever saw!'

'Meanest!'

'Meanest!'

'Meanest!'

'Meanest!'

CHAPTER THREE

As soon as the door shut behind Araminta, tears sprang to Bonny's eyes.

'That's it!' she muttered. 'I'm not staying here!'

Tugging at the door in her turn, she rushed out in the corridor. Where was her mother? She'd find her if she had to burst into every single room in the building, waking the babies in Practical Parenting and sending pens skidding in Copperplate Handwriting.

Hurrying round the corner, she bumped into Toby and his trolley.

'I've got something for you,' he said, and

held out one of her favourite Scoobydoo biscuits.

The stars on the wrapper winked at her temptingly. But Bonny was in no mood to be cheered by treats.

'I don't want it,' she said. 'I can't pay for it, anyway.'

'It's already paid for,' he told her, thrusting it in her hand. And it was only then she noticed the rubber band round it, holding in the folded note.

FOR SALE
One whole day in ghastly,
difficult, slave-driving, no-breaks
Bookkeeping (Advanced).
Will swap for one day being charming.
(Roll on 5pm)
Love, Mum

Bonny unwrapped the Scoobydoo and took a massive bite.

'Thanks,' she said, when her mouth emptied. 'I really, really needed that.'

'I know,' said Toby. And Bonny noticed he was looking at the note in her hand, not the chocolate bar wrapper. She guessed he'd seen

her tears. She didn't care, though. She felt so much better. Good enough to grin at him cheerfully as he gave her a ride on his trolley back to her little room.

If she were the meanest girl Araminta had ever seen, Bonny couldn't help thinking an hour or so later, it was against some pretty stiff competition. In between five-minute visits from each of Mrs Opalene's 'Superstars' explaining exactly what it was she wanted later in the Curls and Purls Show, Bonny switched up some of the microphones dangling from the ceiling in the big mirrored room, and found herself overhearing one catty conversation after another.

Take Miss Stardust and Miss Rosebud. They both seemed nice enough when they were in with Bonny. But, as Serena walked past in the big room, they wrinkled their noses.

Curious, Bonny turned up the microphone over their heads.

'Poo! What's that awful smell?'

'So *sickly*. With just a touch of flower stalks left rotting in a vase.'

'I wonder where it's coming from.' Miss Stardust suddenly pretended to notice Serena glaring. 'Oh, golly!' she said. 'Is it your perfume, Serena? I had no idea. I'm so sorry if Esmeralda and I upset you.'

'Yes, so sorry,' chortled Esmeralda. She turned to Miss Stardust. 'We think it's a nice smell really, don't we, Angelica?'

'Oh, yes!' said Angelica, in a voice that meant, as clear as paint, 'Oh, no, we don't. Really, we think it smells about as pleasant as fresh manure'. But Serena was already hurrying away to the corner of the room, where she stood looking angry and upset for a moment before turning to Pearl, who was standing beside her in a faded old slip, unzipping her big plastic dress bag.

Bonny switched over to the microphone above Pearl's head.

'Pearl!' she heard Serena say. 'That is the nicest dress you've ever worn to Charm School!'

Pearl looked up, baffled. 'But you haven't seen it yet. I'm only just getting it out now.'

Serena's voice dripped with false innocence. 'Isn't that it, what you're wearing?'

'This?' Pearl stared down at the faded, raggedy old slip in which she stood. 'This is some old thing I borrowed from my mum because it doesn't show round the neck when I'm wearing my new outfit.'

'Really?' Serena clapped her hands over her mouth, and acted horrified. 'Oh, I am sorry! I thought it must be your new frock!'

Pearl plucked at it, horrified. 'You didn't mean that, did you? You didn't really think this was the nicest dress I've ever worn?'

Her face was crumpling with unhappiness.

'Of course not!' said Serena in a voice that clearly meant: 'Oh yes, I did. But I had better not admit it'. It was, thought Bonny, exactly the same mean trick to make someone feel bad that Angelica and Esmeralda had just played on Serena herself. Would Pearl catch

on, and tell Serena off for spitefulness? Or would she run in tears to dear, kind, marshmallow-hearted Mrs Opalene? Surely she'd care if all her precious, charming girls began to claw at one another like cats in a sack.

But Mrs Opalene was busy sewing up a fallen length of Cristalle's hem, while comforting weeping Amethyst about a fleck of white in one of her perfect fingernails. So all Pearl did was drift away from Serena, looking very unhappy. Bonny's eyes followed her across the room, till she came to a halt behind Cooki.

For a while Pearl stood watching Cooki brushing her hair in front of the long wide mirror. Then she said kindly, 'Never mind. No-one will notice.'

Anxiously, Cooki spun round. 'No-one will notice what?'

'Your hair.'

'What's wrong with it?'

Again came that same wide-eyed stare and pretend voice of innocence. 'Nothing. Nothing at all. Forget I said anything. It doesn't matter.'

Cooki turned back to the mirror. 'Yes, it does. I want to know what you meant. What

can you see? What's gone wrong with my hair at the back there?'

'Nothing. I *told* you.'

'But you just said—'

'Honestly, Cooki,' Pearl interrupted her sweetly. 'It looks *wonderful*. Especially from the back.' But even through the glass panel, Bonny could see the little smile on Pearl's face that clearly meant, 'But I'm just saying that. It doesn't really'.

And Cooki saw it too.

'It doesn't, does it? It looks silly. Or wrong. Or *something*.' Cooki was panicking. 'What *is* it, Pearl? Tell me!'

'It's nothing. Honestly.' And off floated Pearl, leaving poor Cooki staring in the mirror in dismay. Bonny felt like rushing out of the control room to slap Pearl hard. But then it would only be fair to go and slap Serena, too, for upsetting Pearl. And, after that, she should go after Esmeralda and Angelica for starting the whole thing off. What was the matter with them all? The children in Bonny's first playgroup, when she was three, had all behaved better than this. And what was Mrs Opalene thinking of, caring more about fallen hems and fingernails than about

♥90♥

them all roaming around being hateful to one another? Was this what she meant by having to suffer to be beautiful? But why would it help to have everyone round you feeling totally crummy?

Unless, of course, it was some horrible way of passing the unhappiness on, like a plate that was too hot to hold. It couldn't simply be to do with wanting to be the Supreme Queen and walk off the stage crowned with the glistering tiara. Bonny had been in plenty of competitions. There'd been the canoe race at club camp. And the climb-a-rope contest at the sports centre. And even that poetry speaking final in the school hall. Admittedly, nobody burst into noisy sobs of grief when George's canoe rolled over, tipping him into the water on the last bend. And she doubted if anyone was really very sorry when, in the rope climb, Gillian lost her nerve and her grip at the same time, and cascaded down the rope to the floor. And everyone burst out laughing when Martin forgot the last line of his poem, and just stared bleakly into space. But no-one had actually gone around beforehand, trying to make that sort of thing happen. No-one had taken the time to think

up ways of making all the others lose their confidence, before things even got started.

Perhaps they'd all been too busy. After all, canoeing and climbing ropes and learning poetry use up your energy, and take up time. But things were very different here in Charm School. The problem with trying to win the glistering tiara was that you weren't kept busy actually *doing* things. You were just trying to *be*. Be neat. Be graceful. Be ladylike. Be more beautiful. To end up being the Supreme Queen.

So they had too much time to stand and fret. There was Serena, wrinkling her nose over and over, as if she were still trying to work out if her perfume really did smell like rotting flower stalks. Pearl was fingering her new frock, clearly still wondering if Serena would think it was as horrible as all her other ones. And Cooki, worried stiff, couldn't stop craning to try to see the back of her head in the mirror. Bonny was really relieved when Mrs Opalene stepped up to the microphone, and called them all back to their places in the circle. As Araminta tripped daintily across the room towards her seat, Bonny held up the shawl, to remind her she'd left it. She didn't

want to admit it to herself, but she was really hoping that Araminta would rush back, just for a moment, to fetch it and make peace.

But Araminta just glanced coldly in her direction and then turned away. And then she crossed the circle to whisper something in Suki's ear, and, to Bonny's embarrassment, Suki, too, stared coldly at her through the glass.

The two of them exchanged places, so Araminta had her back to Bonny. Bonny felt terrible. She was quite glad when Mrs Opalene chided both of them.

'Now hurry up, dears, *please*. It's time for our precious *Words About Beauty*.'

Everyone looked delighted. 'Oh, goody!' trilled Amethyst. 'I *love* Words About Beauty!'

'Who'd like to start?' asked Mrs Opalene. 'Who's found some lovely and inspirational words they'd like to share?'

'I have,' said Esmeralda. She stood up, clasped her hands and cocked her head winsomely to the side, and started declaiming:

'*My evening star! Laura, your beauty shines*
As far as yon dark, whispering pines.'

'Enchanting!' cried Mrs Opalene, clasping

her own hands to her glittering bosom. 'Enchanting!'

'Can I be next?' begged Cristalle. 'I have two lines from a lovely poem we did at school.' Like Esmeralda, she clasped her hands before saying it aloud.

'*My lady is a jewel; her pretty eyes*
Sparkle, as on her velvet couch she lies.'

Mrs Opalene's rings flashed as she flattened her hand over her heart. 'Oh, that is nice! *My lady is a jewel*. I do like that. Isn't that nice, girls? Don't you all agree?'

Everyone nodded. Cooki's hand went up. 'I've just remembered one.' Making sure her knees were together and her feet tucked away neatly, she laid her hands in her lap and flicked her hair back, just like Amethyst.

'*Oh, Flora! So well-named! You are a beauteous flower,*
Shimmering in loveliness through every shower.'

'*Shimmering in loveliness,*' repeated Mrs Opalene. 'Doesn't everyone think that's beautiful? I do. I think that's quite inspiring. Thank you, Cooki, dear. Now, who else has a little gem to offer?'

♥94♥

'I do,' said Cindy-Lou, jumping to her feet. 'I found it in a book of verses my granny gave me.'

'Lovely, dear.'

Cindy-Lou spread her hands, and quoted, '*She walks in beauty, like the night.*'

'Oh!' cried Mrs Opalene. She seemed to Bonny to be in the seventh heaven of delight. 'Oh, how we would all like to hear someone saying that of us! *She walks in beauty, like the night.* Wouldn't that be something lovely to aim for? Thank you so much, Cindy-Lou, for sharing that with us. Now, who would like to be next?'

She was still looking hopefully around the circle when Bonny's voice resounded through the loudspeaker.

'So where was she going?'

Hearing her own voice booming back at her, Bonny clapped her hands over her mouth. She hadn't meant to speak aloud, let alone with her own microphone channelled through to the big room. But now Mrs Opalene was peering, a little baffled, towards the glass window.

'Is that you, Miss Sparky? Did you have a question?'

Well, Bonny thought, my mother did buy a ticket. I do have a right to ask one. And to get an answer.

'I was just wonder-ing where she was going,' she told Mrs Opalene.

Mrs Opalene was baffled. 'Who, dear?'

'This woman walk-ing in beauty.'

'*Lady*, I think, dear,' Mrs Opalene reproved her. 'And what does it matter where she was going?'

'I was just interested,' Bonny defended her-self. 'Perhaps Cindy-Lou knows.'

Cindy-Lou didn't. 'The poet doesn't say. He just goes on a bit about how beautiful she was while she was walking there. He doesn't say where she was going, or why.'

'Shame,' Bonny muttered. 'I started out quite liking that one. But that makes it quite as boring as all of the others.'

Everyone stared. Shocked to the core, Mrs Opalene gathered the floaty matching wrap of her gown closer around her shoulders as if

a chill wind had run through the room. 'Sorry, dear? Did I mishear? Could I possibly have heard you say the word "boring" about our lovely, inspirational Words About Beauty?'

'Well, yes,' admitted Bonny, wishing to heaven that she'd kept her mouth shut.

'Beauty that shines like a star?' reverberated Mrs Opalene, as though the switches on the sound panel had all pushed themselves right up to FULL. 'Eyes that sparkle like jewels? Flowers that shimmer in loveliness? You call those—' Her bosom trembled. '—*boring*!'

Bonny was trembling too, now. But still she tried to explain. 'I didn't mean to be rude. It's just that none of those things the poets are writing about actually *do* anything, do they?'

'What do you mean, none of them do anything?'

'Well, they don't,' Bonny said stoutly. 'None of them. Flowers and jewels and stars. They just sit there, looking pretty, and twinkling and glowing. That's all they do, and it must be terribly boring.'

'But they're *beautiful*!'

'Oh, yes,' said Bonny. 'I agree they're all nice to look at. What I'm saying is that it's probably a lot more fun to *look* at them than to *be* them.'

They were all staring at her, open-mouthed.

'After all,' Bonny finished up determinedly. 'Even the lady who could walk in beauty like the night couldn't have been going anywhere very interesting or the poet would have mentioned it.' She was about to switch off the microphone and get on with reading the *Handbook of Sound And Lighting* she'd found in a heap of cassette tapes, when Sarajane spoke up.

'Well, obviously this lady couldn't have been going anywhere very exciting, or she wouldn't have stayed looking nice.'

'That's right,' said Pearl. 'If she'd been climbing up a mountain, she would have got all sweaty.'

'And if she'd been at a funfair, her hair would have been blown about,' said Cristalle.

'And if she'd been on a beach, her make-up would have melted and smudged,' put in Suki.

They were all at it now.

'You can't do very much at all if you want to stay walking in beauty.'

'No, you certainly can't. You might get grubby.'

'Or ladder your tights.'

'Or break a fingernail.'

'Or get stains on your blouse.'

'Or scuff your heels.'

'Or—'

Just as, exasperated, Bonny reached forward to fade out this catalogue of woes, a hand came down to stop her. It was Toby, who had once again slid in silently and was standing behind her.

'Oh, don't turn them off,' he begged. 'I'm listening. This is more exciting than any adventure story. What else could possibly go wrong with their poor clothes?'

He pushed Bonny's fingers so the volume shot up again.

'Or the pleats in your skirt might fall out,'

Angelica was fretting.

'Or you might lose one of your earrings,' warned Amethyst.

'Or your hem might——'

But Bonny couldn't stand it. Jerking her hand under his, she cut Cooki off in mid-wail, and swung round to face him.

'Is it time for lunch yet?' she asked hopefully.

'Nearly. I just came by to pick up your tea cup.'

Their hands collided on the way to pick it up. The cup spun off the ledge, splashing dregs on his jeans.

Clutching his head, the tea boy reeled dramatically round the little back room. 'Oh, no!' he shrilled. 'A spot on my pretty trousers. Now I shall have to go all the way home to change, and I'll be late for the party!'

Seeing Bonny giggle, he stopped, satisfied, and rubbed the dregs of tea into his trousers, where they disappeared. 'Good colour, grey,' he said. 'Hides everything.' He nodded through the glass window. 'Not like all those girly lemons and pinks.'

'Men do wear yellow shirts,' argued Bonny. 'And pink ones.'

'But they don't have to *go* with anything.